A KISS IN SPRING

KISS THE WALLFLOWER, BOOK 3

TAMARA
Gill

COPYRIGHT

A Kiss in Spring
Kiss the Wallflower, Book 3
Copyright © 2019 by Tamara Gill
Cover Art by Wicked Smart Designs
Editor Grace Bradley Editing
Proofread Monique Daoust
All rights reserved.

ISBN 13: 978-0-6487160-1-3

DEDICATION

For those who love Scotland and hot Highlanders...

CHAPTER 1

Highlands Scotland 1805

Sophie Grant dozed halfway between asleep and awake as the carriage continued on north, heading toward a small fishing village near the Isle of Skye. She'd never been to Scotland before and after this arduous journey, she doubted she'd ever go again.

How far away could this little seaside village be? Even so, they'd been traveling for what felt like months, but was in fact only weeks. Granted, they had stopped most nights, and during some breaks, had extended the journey to take in the local attractions or simply to rest both themselves, their driver and the horses.

She settled back into the squabs, luxuriating in the plush velvet seats and highly polished equipage. At least her little sojourn was more comfortable than taking the post. Her new brother-in-law, the Marquess Graham had insisted she use one of his carriages and had sent both a coachman and manservant to ensure her and her maid's safety.

So far they had very little to complain about, except the

never-ending road or that the farther north they traveled the colder it seemed to get.

Sophie had thought spring in Scotland would be warmer than this, but apparently not.

A loud crack sounded and the carriage lurched frighteningly to one side. Sophie slipped off the seat and landed with a thump on the floor, her maid, sleeping on the opposite seat came crashing down on top of her and supplying Sophie with an elbow to the temple.

Distantly she could hear the coachman and manservant talking outdoors before the door swung open and the driver was there, taking in their disheveled appearance.

"Are you hurt, Miss Sophie, Miss May?" he asked, reaching in to help her maid climb off Sophie and regain her footing.

Sophie untangled herself from her dress and managed to slide toward the door and then step out onto the uneven, pothole-filled dirt road.

"Well, I think we can at least say why our wheel has broken in two." Sophie glanced at the sad wooden wheel lying beside the carriage, several spikes missing completely, possibly on the road behind them before the wheel collapsed under the carriage's weight.

"We're not far from the town Moy. I can leave you here with Thomas and go and fetch a new vehicle or we can all walk to town and I'll return later to pick up Thomas and collect your belongings."

"We'll walk with you, Peter. If you're happy to wait here with the carriage, Thomas?" Sophie asked, not wanting him to stay here alone if he did not feel comfortable.

"I'm armed, Miss Sophie. I'll wait here until Peter returns. Town is not so far away, I can see smoke from some chimneys already."

Sophie looked north up the road and true enough, there were little swirls of smoke floating up in the air behind a small rise in the road. "Oh, we're not far at all." She reached into the carriage and looked for her reticule. Finding it on the floor, she picked it up and turned back to their little group. "Shall we?"

The walk into the village took no longer than half an hour and soon enough they were walking past the few cottages the village sported. A small sign pronounced the town to be Moy. A few of the locals came out to stare and some welcomed them with a friendly smile or wave.

"Do you think there is an inn in town, Miss Sophie? That carriage wheel will take some days to repair," her maid, Gretel, asked, looking about the town with a less-than-pleased visage.

Sophie took account of the sleepy village, fear that there would be no inn washed over her. "I hope so. We need to secure rooms for some days and wait out the repairs. We're in no rush after all, and the carriage being Lord Graham's, I'd prefer to wait for it to be fixed than leave it here. But there doesn't seem to be a lot of people living here."

"I'm sure all will work out, Miss Sophie. Do not worry," Peter said, throwing her an easy smile.

They came to a crossroad and thankfully spied what looked like the local inn. It was made of stone and a thatch roof. A carriage sat parked to the side, and a young stable lad placed luggage at its back.

Sophie hoped that it was a place travelers could stay, or they would need to leave Marquess Graham's carriage here and travel on without it. If there was a carriage they could procure, in any case.

Peter led the way into the taproom, which had some men seated at the bar drinking ale. A barman with a long, graying beard came up to them and leaned upon the counter. "What

3

can I help ye with?" he asked, taking each of them in before turning back to Peter.

"We're after two rooms if you have them available. Our carriage has broken a wheel outside of town and I'll need a cart to collect our luggage, if you please."

The barman rubbed his bearded jaw. "Ach, we can help ye with that to be sure, but I only have one room left, we're not officially an inn, but we can help ye out since our guests overnight are leaving as we speak. If you're willing, sir, I can put you up in the stables on a cot."

Peter nodded. "That will be fine. We'll need two cots as I have left a manservant with the carriage."

The barman stood, and Sophie found herself looking up at the towering gentleman. He was as tall as he was wide, his fiery-red hair and stature perfect for the position he held. "No trouble, sir, that can be arranged." He bellowed out for a woman named Bridget and within a minute a young woman bustled into the room, her hair askew and her apron covered in cooking stains. She smiled at each of them and Sophie smiled back.

"Show these ladies upstairs and have Alfie set up two cots in the stable. We'll also be needing the cart hitched."

"Of course, Father," she said, opening a small door in the bar and coming out to them. "If ye will follow me, my ladies. I'll show ye to your room."

"We'll be in the stable, Miss Sophie. I'll have Thomas bring in your luggage when we return with it."

"Thank you, Peter." Sophie followed the young woman up a narrow flight of stairs, stepping to the side when another young woman carrying a bucket and dressed in similar clothing to Bridget passed them on their way down.

They made their way along a passageway before coming to a room at the very end. The young woman unlocked the door with a key and swung it wide open.

"Here is ye room, my ladies. I'll have hot water and linens brought up straightaway. There is a private parlor downstairs if ye do not wish to eat in your lodgings, but ye do have a small table and two chairs if ye wish to."

Sophie walked into the room, taking in the double bed that looked clean and inviting. The curtains were new and there were flowers on a small table. A fire burned in the grate and the room was warm and welcoming.

"This is lovely," she said, stripping off her shawl and throwing it on the bed along with her reticule. "For an inn that doesn't trade in accommodation, it is very well-kept and presentable."

The young woman blushed at the compliment and her chin rose slightly with pride. "Aye, we're very lucky. The inn is owned by our local laird Brice Mackintosh but run by my father. His sister is responsible for the recent refurbishment of this room. 'Tis the only one we have since the building is so small. The few patrons we get here always appreciate a clean bed and good meal."

"That they do," Gretel said, sliding back the curtain to look outside. "May we order an early dinner? We've been traveling all day and I have to admit to being quite famished."

"Of course," the young woman said. "We're serving roast chicken and beef stew this evening, which do you prefer?"

At the mention of food Sophie's stomach rumbled. "I'll have the stew please, and a pot of tea if possible."

"I'll have the same, thank you," Gretel said, pulling off her shawl and laying it on a chair by the fire.

The young woman bobbed a quick curtsy and started for the door. "I'll be back shortly, my lady."

"You may call me Miss Grant."

"Aye, of course. I shall return, Miss Grant." The door closed behind the young woman and Sophie stripped off her gloves, placing them on the mantel as she warmed herself before the fire.

"What a lovely inn and so accommodating. Certainly a much more pleasant place than some of the English ones we've stayed in."

Gretel nodded, coming to sit at the small table. She pulled off her gloves before yawning. "I'm dreadfully tired. A nice meal will be just what we need, along with a good night's rest."

The warmth from the fire slowly penetrated Sophie's bones and she shut her eyes, reveling in being warm and out of the jarring carriage. "I think we'll be here for several days. Perhaps there is a carriage-maker in the town who can repair the wheel, but I'm doubtful. I should say it will have to be brought up with the post from London."

"But that could take weeks," Gretel said, her eyes wide with alarm. "Although the lodgings are very comfortable, whatever will we do for all that time? Is there anything about to look at? I think I could count on one hand how many cottages were here."

Sophie walked to the window and stared out at the street, spotting a blacksmith and a small shop of some kind, but from where she stood she couldn't make it out.

"We'll ask tomorrow what there is to see and do here. I'm sure we can pass the time well enough, and anyway, we've been on the road for so long, a little break from travel will do us good."

Gretel nodded. "I'm sure you're right."

A light knock sounded on the door before it opened and Bridget entered, carrying a tray of tea and biscuits, along with a small bowl of cream and jam. She placed it down on the table. "The tea has just been poured, so perhaps let it sit for a little while before taking a cup."

"Thank you, it looks delicious."

"I'll bring dinner up in about ten minutes. Cook is just finishing it up now."

Sophie smiled at her, seating herself at the table. "Thank you, that is very good of you."

"You're welcome, Miss Grant."

When they were alone once again, Gretel went about putting cream and jam onto the biscuits along with preparing the tea for them to drink. They sat in silence for a time as they ate and enjoyed the refreshing drink, both lost in their thoughts.

"The young woman said that the inn is owned by the local laird and his sister. Perhaps we can visit with them. I've never met a Scottish laird before. He may live in a castle," Sophie teased. "I know how much you enjoy old houses."

Gretel nodded as she took a rather large bite of her biscuit. "I've always thought that Scottish lairds lived in castles, so I would expect nothing else," she mumbled.

Sophie chuckled. "I think I understood what you said, but really, Gretel, maybe smaller bites in the future."

Gretel smiled, her eyes bright with laughter. "Of course," she mumbled yet again.

Sophie poured herself another cup of tea. Being stuck in this sleepy but quaint town would surely be diverting enough to while away their time until the carriage was repaired. The landscape alone was beautiful, the forest and surrounding rugged hills drew the eye and beckoned one to explore. Maybe if they hired a local guide, they could picnic at a location the locals enjoyed.

Yes, they could have ended up stranded in much worse locations than Moy and they would make the best of their time while they were here.

CHAPTER 2

The following morning after breaking their fast in their small room, Sophie made her way outside with Gretel, walking into an inn yard that housed their carriage, a few horses and little else. "Come, we'll walk through the town and see what we can find." Maybe the shop she'd seen sold pastries. She'd always been fond of sweets, although she rarely had them as a child. There were never enough funds for such treats. But now that she had the means, she and Gretel often enjoyed sugary pastries in front of the fire before bed.

They passed very few people on the street. She supposed because the town was not so very far from Inverness, it was only logical that travelers continued on and broke their journey there. They too would have done the same had the carriage wheel not decided to break off.

The air was fresh and she pulled her shawl closer about her shoulders. She supposed she really ought to start wearing her coat as they traveled farther north.

She spied their driver speaking to the local blacksmith, no doubt about their wheel, but the man's constant shaking of his head didn't bode well for them to be out and back on the road traveling toward Skye sooner rather than later.

They came to the shop she'd seen yesterday and she was pleased to see they sold not only food but houseware and linens. Sophie stared in through the shop windows at the few items they displayed there. Her mouth watered at the sight of a queen and seed cake. She glanced through the glass and felt her eyes widen at the sight of a tall, quite imposing figure who stood at the counter. He had his back to her, the strong, straight lines beneath his shirt revealing to all what a lovely, lean and muscular figure he had beneath that thin article of clothing.

But it was his kilt, made of a green, woven wool within a darker green pattern that had her biting her lip. She'd never seen a highlander before, but that was certainly what he was. Straight from the mythical legends this area was famous for.

His hair was long for a man and large curls that looked wind-kissed or mussed from bed sport sat about his shoulders. She grinned at her own imagining of how his hair was so unkept, but still it did not stop her from wanting to run her fingers through the coppery locks.

She clenched her hands at her sides, reminding her she was wearing her kid-leather gloves and would not be able to feel him even if she were to be so bold. Not that she would, but he was nice to look at in any case.

"Are we going to go inside, Miss Sophie?" Gretel asked, shuffling on her feet and rubbing her arms to warm them. "I'm freezing. I don't know how we'll survive going farther north. Even this far up in Scotland is cold enough."

Sophie nodded distractedly, her attention fixed on the Scot being served by a young woman with a white apron over her pink, woolen gown. "Yes, of course."

They entered and a little bell dinged above them. Sophie glanced up at the brass bell before looking back toward the counter and the breath in her lungs held. She felt her mouth pop open with an intake of much-needed air as the green, hard stare of the highlander took his fill of her.

Gretel cleared her throat at her back and Sophie remembered to step forward, moving toward the counter and trying with all the willpower ever afforded to her to keep her attention on the pastries she intended to purchase.

Her cheeks burned and she could feel his gaze tracing over her, before he turned back to the serving girl. "How much do I owe ye, Rhona?"

His voice was deep, smooth like liquid chocolate, and the shiver that ran up her spine had nothing to do with the frigid air in this part of the world.

Sophie glanced toward where he stood and watched as the serving girl leaned over the counter, her ample advantages in full view of anyone standing in the store. "Two farthings please, Laird Mackintosh."

Laird? The highlander reached into his sporran and passed the woman some coin.

"Thank ye, Rhona. I'll see ye next week."

The young woman tittered and Sophie bit back a smile at her infatuation with the man, not that Sophie could blame her. He was not at all what she was expecting to find this far north in the wild Scottish highlands.

He turned toward Sophie and caught her eye and for a moment she could not look away. His compelling eyes drew her in and she turned, following his progress as he made his way out the door, before striding past the shop front windows and disappearing up the street.

"He's a fine laird, if ever there was one," the young woman behind the counter sighed to an older lady who'd come to stand beside her. The elder shushed her and Sophie stepped up to the counter, ensuring she was served by the younger girl.

"May I order two queen cakes and a loaf of bread with seeds on top, please?" she asked. They were quite alone now, Gretel waiting patiently behind her and the older woman in the store serving another customer.

"Of course ye can." She busied herself packing up the pastries, wrapping them in wax paper.

"Did I hear you say that the gentleman that you just served was a laird?" Sophie met the woman's widened eyes and pinkened cheeks and smiled. "He looks very friendly," she continued, hoping to gain some information.

"Oh, aye, it was and he's a Scottish earl as well. He lives in Moy Castle half a mile northeast from here, not far from the banks of Loch Moy. He often comes into town to enjoy my mama's cooking. Honey biscuits are his favorite."

He had a sweet tooth, but then, so did she so she could not fault him on that. Not that she was looking to find fault with the man in any case. It was simply a little odd that a man of his size and stature, who looked like a Scottish warlord, would come into a bakery and buy sweets. She smiled, handing over her payment and taking the small parcel from the shopgirl.

"Thank you. Have a good day," Sophie said.

"You too, my lady," the young woman called out as they left.

They made their way outside, and Sophie took in the small village and the large, rocky outcrops of the highlands that dwarfed the town in the background. It was certainly an idyllic location, but even now in the middle of spring the air was chilly, the ground still damp underfoot.

They walked along the road for a time, looking at the many cottages, some that reminded Sophie of the village that she grew up in. It did not take them long to come to the edge of town where nothing but forest and a waterway greeted them.

"There is a bridge and what looks like a path leading up the hill, Miss Sophie. Shall we explore a little?"

The day was still young after all, they had a little food with them now, and they had their woolen cloaks. Sophie nodded, seeing no reason why they could not.

"Yes, perhaps it'll lead up to a lookout over the town." They had little else to do to fill the time before the carriage was repaired and Sophie was not ready to go back to their room at the inn just yet. A little fresh air and exercise would do them good.

They walked for a time in silence, both lost in their own thoughts. Every now and then Gretel or Sophie would point out a splendid view, or a plant that caught their eye.

The wind whipped at Sophie's hair and she pulled her shawl up over her head to keep it from blinding her. "The wind is picking up, Gretel. We should probably head back soon."

Gretel stopped, pointing ahead of her. "We're almost there, just a little farther."

The hill they climbed was steeper than Sophie first thought, and the breath in her lungs burned as she continued to climb. The ground underfoot was rocky in parts, and slippery in others and nerves pooled in her stomach that perhaps their morning walk was beginning to look like a bad idea.

With that thought, her foot landed on a plant that hid a stone. It slipped out from under her and she toppled forward, coming down onto the ground and slamming into a boulder. An acrid taste entered her mouth when she bit her tongue. Sophie sat up, her vision swimming a little.

"Miss Sophie!" Gretel said, running to her as best she could and kneeling before her. Her friend fumbled in her pocket and brought out a handkerchief, pushing it against her forehead.

Sophie hissed in a breath at the sting of her friend's touch. "Ouch, that hurts."

"You're bleeding. You hit your head and you're bleeding more than you should be."

Sophie swiped at her cheek, glanced down, and gasped at the amount of blood on her fichu and gown. "Oh my Lord, I'm going to bleed to death."

Gretel bit back a smile, pushing harder against her wound. "While I do not think it is as bad as all that, I do think I should fetch help to carry you down. I don't want you to faint and hit your pretty head again."

Sophie glanced at Gretel. It was just like her friend to try to make a small joke in the middle of a disaster. She sighed. "Fine. I'll sit here if you think it's best, but I'm sure I could make it." She looked down the path that they had walked. It was an awfully long way back down.

"I'll be back as fast as I can. Do not move," Gretel said, and then she was gone.

Sophie watched her disappear down the side of the hill before she was out of sight. She pressed against the wound on her forehead, dabbing at it a little to see if it was still bleeding. A light thumping started at her temples and she shuffled over to a large boulder and tried to protect herself from the wind.

How long she sat there she did not know, but as the hours passed and the afternoon grew darker and colder, she slipped into sleep on the craggy ground, heedless that her gown was growing ever more damp by the minute.

*

*B*rice Mackintosh had better things to do than rescue women who were foolhardy enough to walk up hills during this time of year. The ground was damp and slippery and the lass was lucky she'd not broken anything else other than that thick head of hers.

After having been waved down by a young woman running from the bridge that led to the summer lookout over the town, she'd then gone on to explain that her mistress had fallen and needed help down the hill.

Brice looked at the sleeping woman. The once-white handkerchief she'd been using to press against her head wound was lying in the mud and her wound gaped, the congealed blood seeping slowly down her forehead.

He cringed. The injury would need stitching and that in itself alleviated some of his anger at being waylaid. He kneeled beside her, reaching out to shake her shoulder. "Miss. Wake up, miss…" He shook her shoulder a little more and this time her eyes fluttered open.

Her lashes were long and dark, and yet her hair was sun-kissed. Whatever hairstyle she'd had this morning had long ago fallen out.

He stared at her as she sat up, reaching out and taking her hand to help her. She clutched at her head and he cringed when she did. "I'm Brice Mackintosh. I'm going to carry ye down to the town. Will ye let me, lass?" he asked.

She glanced at him, confusion in her gaze, but she nodded, trying to stand.

Brice stood and, reaching down, swooped her into his arms and started back toward the village. Her arms went about his neck and she gave out a sweet little yelp at his manhandling. She smelled of lavender soap and her hair even better, like wild berries and fruit.

The wind blew it into his face, and he fought to keep it out the way as he made his way down the hill. She would be tall, he could tell, and carrying her against his chest put into focus how very womanly she was. Her bottom hit his stomach and his hand sat just beneath her breast as he carried her—both locations on her person that felt ample and lush.

He frowned, reminding himself that being here, helping this lass would make him late for the dinner party he was holding for his potential future wife. His sister would accuse him of being late because she believed him to be indifferent to Elspeth. A truth that even he acknowledged even though he'd never tell his sister such a thing. He glanced down at the lass and caught her studying him.

"How are you doing down there?" He took in her wound. It still wept, but had at least stopped bleeding. As for her appearance, it was disheveled to say the least. Half her face sported dry blood, and her golden locks too were a little stained and clumped from the wound.

"Your friend said you're staying at the inn. I'll have a doctor sent straightaway over to you when we return."

"Thank you," she said, speaking at last. She frowned up at him, studying him as if he were an oddity. "Are you the laird I saw in the shop earlier today?"

Realization struck him and he stumbled a little. That was where he'd seen her before! As per usual, his daily walk and honey biscuit purchase had today been a little less banal than it normally was. And it was because of this lass in his arms. "Aye."

He'd heard the door to the shop open, but it wasn't until he'd glanced to see who had stepped inside that his body had stilled at the sight of her. She was all golden beauty. Her eyes so wide and blue that they would make even the sky envious. He'd stared at her, unable to look away before he'd realized his mistake and had turned back to Rhona to finish being served.

In Moy there were few women who looked like the one in his arms and it had merely been a shock to see anyone. She was a Sassenach as well, and not worth his time.

15

He was to marry a Scottish lass, Elspeth Brodie in fact. A woman who was as robust and capable as anyone he knew. The fact that she'd never raised one ounce of attraction in him was beside the point.

Many marriages were based on friendship and they were friends…most of the time.

Finally they made the bridge that separated the walk up the hill and the town. Her friend stood waiting for them, a deep frown on her brow as she worked her hands before her in worry.

Brice sent her a comforting smile, trying to put her at ease. The young woman visibly relaxed upon spying them.

"You're very strong. There are few who would be able to carry me all this way and without even puffing." She studied him and he refused to meet her gaze lest she see just how very fascinating he found her.

"I work. I should imagine you know very little of the trade." She stiffened in his arms and he inwardly cringed. There was no need to be so curt and opinionated about the lass in his arms. For all he knew she did work, although her fine clothing and hands that were soft against his neck told him otherwise.

She was no trouble to carry, in fact, she weighed very little, although her close proximity did give way to thoughts that he should not be having, not with this lass at least. Brice reminded himself that he was expected to marry Elspeth. A woman who was native to this land and wouldn't fall over on the craggy mountaintops and cut her head open like this lass.

He came up to her friend and helped the woman in his arms stand. "I'll help ye to the inn and then fetch the doctor. He'll have ye fixed up soon enough."

Brice took her arm, helping her forward. "Thank you again for assisting me. My name is Sophie Grant, by the way." She stopped and held out her hand.

He stared at it a moment before reaching down, clasping it and bowing over it a little. Something in his gut twisted watching her and he turned back toward the inn. He needed to get her back and settled. There was much to do at home, what with the dinner this evening. His sister would no doubt be flustered and bossing everyone about since he wasn't there to keep her in check.

Not that he ever could.

"I'm Brice Mackintosh," he said at length, nodding to the few locals who glanced their way and stopped to watch what their laird was doing with a bloodied woman.

He supposed the sight didn't place him in a favorable light, but what could he do under the circumstances? He could not have left her there. The drop in temperature alone overnight would've taken her life, not to mention it wasn't his nature to turn from people in need.

They made the inn and Brice, with the aid of the tavern staff, helped Miss Grant to her room, her friend fussing to ensure hot water and linens were brought up straightaway.

Their room was the only one available for guests, and Brice glanced about, spying the large leather traveling cases.

He helped Miss Grant to the chair before the fire, ensuring she was sitting before he stepped back. "I'll have a doctor sent immediately. I wish ye well, Miss Grant."

She glanced up at him. Was that a flicker of disappointment in her gaze? Surely not. He was imagining things now?

The other woman came over to him, taking his hand and squeezing it. "Thank you ever so much, my lord. We're so very appreciative of your help. I do not know what I would've done had you not stopped."

Brice backed toward the door. "Think nothing of it, lass. Yer friend will be better soon enough."

She smiled, following him, before shutting the door quietly behind him as he made his way down the passage. At the tavern, he stopped to greet John Oates, a tenant of his before heading outdoors.

A man bustled up to him, his fine clothing and pale skin gave him the air of an Englishman. He sighed. What was it today with the English needing a Scot's help?

"My lord, I don't know how to thank you enough for the help with Miss Grant." The man clasped his hand, shaking it vigorously. "I was out, you see. Our carriage is broken and being repaired and I did not know Miss Grant had been injured. I do not know what I would've said to her sister had something happened to her." The man worked his cap in his hand and Brice waved his thanks aside. "I was more than willing to help. Ye have no reason to worry. She's safe and sound in her room now."

The man sighed, nodding. "Thank you. I shall let my master know of your kindness. It will not be forgotten."

Brice frowned at the mention of his employer. "Master?"

"Oh yes, Miss Grant is the sister-in-law to the Marquess Graham."

For a moment Brice couldn't think of anything to say. She was nobility, or at least, related to English peers.

If that was the case, what in the hell had a woman of rank —even if only by marriage—been doing walking around the wilds of the Scottish highlands without a manservant? Or for that matter, staying at an inn with only a woman servant in her room?

Moy Inn may be quiet and the only accommodation in town, but it was far from safe for an unprotected woman. There were many riffraff who passed through and could've assaulted or stolen from them.

"Dinna let her wander around Moy alone, 'tis not safe for her or her servant." Who, no doubt, the other young woman fussing about Miss Grant's skirts was.

"Of course, my lord. Thank you."

Brice left then, striding to the doctor's residence only some houses away and paying for his services to the young woman. He then started back to where he'd left his horse. By the time he hoisted himself into the saddle, drizzle had settled in over the town and with it a decided chill to the air. He pulled part of his kilt over his shoulders and pushed his horse into a trot, needing to get back home sooner rather than later.

He had a dinner to host for his possible future wife. He sighed at the thought. He supposed he'd have to start courting Elspeth Brodie soon. The obligation held little desire for him. The image of Miss Sophie Grant flashed before his eyes and he let himself remember her soft, curvy flesh against his. The smell of lavender and fruits of all things sweet and succulent.

Pity his future was not so alluring to his palate.

CHAPTER 3

*S*ophie woke with only the slightest headache the following day. The doctor had come, and forced her to endure two stitches up high on her forehead, which she would never forgive him for. The pain of having a needle threaded through skin was not to ever be borne again and Sophie had promised herself no more hillside walks. From now on she would keep to flat, dry ground. Not steep, rocky, damp ground that was abundant in these parts.

"Would you be up to having breakfast in the parlor downstairs, Miss Sophie? The day has dawned very bright and the room gets the lovely morning sun."

Sophie slipped on her slippers. She walked to the window and looked out over the street. Again the town was a hive of activity and just as Gretel said, the day looked much more congenial to outings than it did yesterday.

"Yes, I feel well enough." She checked the bandage on her head. "I'll have to wear my jockey bonnet to cover the bandage. If I tip it a little over my brow and to one side, I don't think anyone will see the injury." She picked up her hat and sat it over her hair, tying it simply at the back of her head.

"I think that'll work well, miss." Gretel checked her over and, clasping her shawl and handing it to her, she opened the door. "Shall we?"

They enjoyed a lovely breakfast of toast and kippers, along with a nice hot pot of tea. The cook had even placed some bacon and eggs on the platter.

A little while later, Sophie slumped back in the chair, not able to eat another bite. "Shall we go for a walk?"

Gretel glanced at her, shock etched onto her face. "Do you think that's wise after yesterday?"

Sophie laughed. She supposed her friend had a point. Yesterday had not been either of their best moments. "I want to go look at the little river that runs behind this town. We'll not go far, I promise. Will you join me?"

Gretel nodded, standing. "Of course, there isn't much else for us to do."

Unfortunately that was true. Sophie stood, and they started out of the inn, heading toward the river. For some hours they walked along the banks, sitting when they needed a break, and talking to the few locals who were fishing at certain locations along the way.

"I must admit that this town really is quite lovely, even if it is terribly small."

Gretel nodded. They sat along the bank in long grass, simply watching the clouds pass over the highlands in the distance.

"You must send word to Miss Anderson. She'll be expecting you in a few days and she may worry when we don't arrive."

Sophie nodded. "I shall pen a letter tonight to her and we'll send it with the morning post. I should not think we will be here too much longer in any case. Peter said they were able to get a wheel from Inverness."

"Miss Grant! Hello! Miss Grant is that you?"

Sophie turned at the female voice calling to her, or hollering would be a better term. From the direction they had walked came a young woman, dressed in a tartan skirt and white shirt, her shawl was wool and her hair was a simple plait at her back. She smiled and waved and for a moment Sophie was unsure what to do. Should she wave back to the strange woman who obviously knew her name, or wait and see?

She stood, brushing down her gown and decided that the lady looked harmless enough. What with her wide smile and bright eyes, she was obviously no threat.

She came up to them, panting heavily, and she clasped her midriff, smiling at them and yet unable to speak due to her exhaustion.

"Are you well?" Sophie asked when after a moment the woman still had not caught her breath.

"Apologies, Miss Grant," she said, panting. "I've been trying to catch up to ye. You walk very fast for a Sassenach."

Sophie raised her brow. For an Englishwoman she walked fast? She didn't know whether to be proud or offended by the remark. "Can I help you with something?"

The woman nodded. "Aye, I'm Elizabeth Mackintosh, Laird Mackintosh's sister. I think ye met my brother yesterday."

The lady reached out and took Sophie's hand, shaking it with vigor. "It's very nice to meet you. Was there something wrong, or is there something you need?" she asked, unsure why the woman was tracking them down.

Elizabeth chuckled, pushing back a lock of hair that had fallen over her face. The laird's sister was just as handsome as her brother, except her hair was a fiery red, which Sophie could well agree suited the woman's exuberance and zest for life.

"Oh nay, nothing to worry about. My brother informed me ye were from London and the Marquess Graham's sister-in-law. I know the marquess well. He's a mutual friend of the family I stayed with during my coming out many years ago. Knowing this, I coudna allow ye to stay a moment longer at the inn. Ye must come and stay with us at Moy Castle."

Sophie glanced at Gretel, who in turn stared bright-eyed at Elizabeth. The thought of staying with the laird of the area was tempting, and not only because the accommodations would be a little more roomy and comfortable, but also quiet. The inn was terribly noisy to all hours of the night. The few locals who did live in the village seemed quite in love with the taproom. "We would not wish to intrude."

"Och, 'tis not an intrusion at all. We have ample room and plenty to keep ye occupied. I understand yer carriage is being repaired?" Elizabeth Mackintosh shrugged. "I see no reason why ye shoulda come and stay."

Sophie looked to Gretel and with a small nod, she came to a decision. "Very well, thank you, Miss Mackintosh. We'd be delighted to be your guests."

he following day Sophie, with the help of a servant, stepped out of the carriage that the laird had sent to collect them in Moy. She glanced up at the castle structure, a large, square tower sitting pride and center. The details about the roof were ornate and gothic in appearance and to Sophie did not represent what she'd always assumed a clan stronghold would look like.

Not that Scotland was allowed to have clans, such as they were hundreds of years ago. Even so, the families that had survived Culloden still bore the names, the independence and pride of their people.

Elizabeth bustled out of the hall, coming over to them. "So glad you're here, and just in time for lunch. Come, I'll show ye to yer rooms so ye may freshen up before we eat."

They made their way indoors and Sophie felt her eyes grow wide at the size of the home. The entrance housed a library to one side and another room of equal mass on the other. Settees, a piano and other opulent furniture littered the space and oozed history and a well-used home.

Elizabeth started up the central staircase that was large and imposing like the house itself, its dark oak drew the eye and all but shouted wealth and power in these lands.

She followed Miss Mackintosh upstairs to the second floor. Turning right, Elizabeth strode down a long hall. "In there is the smaller drawing room, and if you follow me down the second passage," she said, turning yet again, "here you'll find the guest bedrooms. I also sleep in the farthest room down the hall here as it's a corner room and has great views over the park from both windows. My brother occupies the other wing. I'll show ye that tomorrow."

"Where shall I stay, Miss Mackintosh?" Gretel asked, her eyes as wide as Sophie felt hers were. The home was even larger than the marquess and her sister Louise's country estate. One could possibly become lost in all the rooms and corridors.

"There is a little adjoining chamber with a bed, side table and closet in through here for you," Elizabeth said. "You may order your meals in here or join the servants below stairs. I've instructed the housekeeper either will be acceptable. Her name is Mrs. Kenny."

"Thank you," Gretel said, seemingly pleased with her accommodations.

"Dinner is at eight sharp and we always dine in the great

hall. That is downstairs," Elizabeth said, looking over the room before starting toward the door. "Once you're settled, please come down to have luncheon. We're having a simple buffet today, so no need to feel ye have to be there straight-away for serving."

"Thank you," Sophie said, turning to Gretel as Elizabeth closed the door behind her, leaving them alone.

"This house is out of a dream. The Mackintoshes must be very rich indeed," Gretel said, walking into her room, her voice muffled.

Sophie turned, taking in what was to be her space. Again, all dark woods, rich Aubusson rugs, windows that ran from floor to ceiling. The view of the lands drew her eye and Sophie looked out onto the park. She could well understand why Elizabeth wanted a room with two windows over-looking such a landscape.

Large elm and oak trees spotted the lands, native grasses were left to grow wild and there was only the smallest area of lawn that surrounded the house itself before giving way to nature. Movement caught Sophie's eye and she spied a stag, munching on the undergrowth, perfectly content. She could well understand that. With the view from here, her room was far and beyond better than the inn's.

Sophie turned and sat on the window ledge. An imposing fireplace, opposite the bed, dominating the other side of the room. Even from where she was, she could feel the warmth emanating from it.

"I think we'll be very comfortable here."

Gretel bustled over to her. "Come, Miss Sophie, I'll get you ready for luncheon, fix up your hair to hide your wound, and then you best head downstairs. I'll unpack our things while you're gone and have my lunch in here today. That way I'll have you organized for this evening's entertainments, whatever they may be."

Sophie nodded, sitting at the dressing table while Gretel went about fixing her pinned hair and ensuring her gown was suitable for lunch.

How things had changed. Only a few years ago she was living in the small village of Sandbach with her aunt and brother. Louise away working as a lady's companion, and now she was a marchioness. Beyond happy and in love with her husband and taking care of her and Stephen as she'd always had.

To be in the Laird Mackintosh's home as a guest was simply too fantastical to imagine, and yet, here she was. Louise had made her promise to behave and enjoy her time away from London and this was certainly a lot of fun.

She just hoped the other house guests were as welcoming as Elizabeth Mackintosh had been.

"There, all done, Miss Sophie."

Sophie glanced at herself in the mirror. Her morning gown of rose pink was the height of fashion in London and because they did not have far to travel out to the hall this morning, she'd forgone wearing a traveling gown.

At least by doing so she was ready to dine. "Thank you, Gretel. I shall see you after lunch." She took a calming breath, the pit of her stomach twisting at the thought of seeing the laird once again.

To see if he was as handsome as her mind told her he was or if she'd simply hit her head so hard that it had left her confused and muddled of mind.

CHAPTER 4

*B*rice sat at the head of the table and spooned mouthful after mouthful of food as he tried to hasten his departure from lunch. His sister sat quiet, a small smile playing about her lips and his eyes narrowed. What was she up to?

His attention snapped to the end of the table where Elspeth Brodie, his intended if his family had their way, sat and ate. Her expression was blank, displeased even. Was there something wrong with the food? "Is the food not to yer liking, Elspeth?" he asked, catching her eye and throwing her a small smile.

She looked back at him as if he were an inanimate object not worth her time. "Nay, the broth is too salty for my palate. Ye should have a word with yer cook. It seems she's inadequate."

Brice nodded, even though he had no intention of talking to Mrs. Ross. She was one of the best in the area, and made the most delicious-tasting kippers anyone north of the border. She wouldn't be going anywhere.

He spooned more broth into his mouth. The thought of

meals such as these for the rest of his life, of a wife who disliked his cook and his home if he were to guess, didn't raise too much excitement in his blood. Why his parents had wished for such a union was beyond him. Just because one was friends with another clan did not mean such unions were necessary. He stirred his broth. But he knew the reason why. Debts must be paid and even if the fiscal ones were long over, the moral one still remained.

The door to the hall opened and every muscle in his body seized at the sight of the woman who strode into the room. He gaped at her, spoon partway to his mouth as she started toward Elizabeth.

His sister stood, gesturing to a chair beside her. "Everyone, this is Sophie Grant from London. She's the sister-in-law of Marquess Graham. Sophie, this is our neighbor and friend Miss Elspeth Brodie and of course my brother whom you met yesterday."

Elspeth took in Sophie's appearance and smiled, sitting up and paying a little more attention to what was going on about her. Brice watched his intended for a moment, wondering why Sophie would spark such a reaction, certainly nothing else had.

Sophie glanced at him, her tentative smile slipping a little. He schooled his features to one of disinterest. "Welcome, Miss Grant. I can only gather from your appearance here this afternoon that my sister has invited ye to stay?"

Miss Grant glanced at Elizabeth and he knew his sister had not told her that he knew nothing of their coming here. "Rest easy, Miss Grant, ye're more than welcome."

He sighed, not sure how he was going to go about the house now with her under its roof. She was beyond beautiful, and even the little cut on her forehead that her maid had tried to mask with her hairstyle didn't detract from the fact that he liked what he saw.

Brice stood, going to the server for more food, needing to distract himself. All would be well. He'd be polite, show her about the grounds and be friendly. Just because she was one of the most handsome people he'd met did not mean that they would get along as well. Not to mention Elspeth was here with the full knowledge that if he should ask she was to say yes to his proposal.

He slumped back in his chair, his appetite gone. For a time he pushed the bacon and fried egg about his plate and let the conversation about him continue without his input, until he heard Sophie's sweet voice and his gaze was pulled away from his food.

"What did you think of the house, Miss Grant?" Elspeth asked. Brice glanced at her, having not heard such interest in her tone for all the years he'd known her.

"Very well, Miss Brodie. The house is beautiful and the grounds are marvelous. I said to my maid before coming down that even Luke and Louise would be envious."

Pride filled him at her words and he found his lips twitching.

"Do you really? I always thought Moy Castle quite cold and masculine. 'Tis too grand for my blood and that of our Scottish ancestors too I believe."

Brice stared nonplussed at Elspeth. The woman was daft, just like both her parents.

"Ye disagree, Miss Grant," Elspeth stated matter-of-fact.

"I do," Sophie said, taking a sip of her wine. "It is no secret that I along with my siblings grew up with very little. We are not nobility, even though my sister has married into that sphere. A house like this, grand, old, full of history and family memories is something I know naught of. We lived in a cottage growing up in a small village in northern England.

"My aunt took us in after our parents died, and even though she loved us, we were never really a family after that.

29

At least not one that was together until Louise married the marquess. I would've loved to have grown up in a home like this. A residence that has seen generations of my blood before. A sanctuary that could never be taken away from you. A place you'd always have as home."

Brice started when his sister clapped, nodding at her words. "I agree, Miss Grant," she said. "Moy Castle has been here hundreds of years and will be for hundreds more. 'Tis a shame that others are not so fortunate."

"Well, we'll see what ye think of the castle after a cold winter. The rooms I grant ye are warm, but 'tis a dreary, dark place. If ye're ever in Brodie land, ye must come to call, Miss Grant. Ye're more than welcome at my home."

Miss Grant smiled at Elspeth and his gut clenched. If the house was so dark and dreary as per Elspeth's opinion, then a smile from Miss Grant surely made it brighter.

"I would like that, thank you. Maybe on our return to London I shall call."

"Och, aye, that's right. Brice did mention that ye were not staying in the area long. Ye have a friend in Scotland that ye were traveling to see."

"I do. We went to the same school in Sandbach for a time before her family moved back to Skye. Her father is a tenant farmer for a laird up there."

Brice continued to eat, but didn't engage himself in the conversation. Miss Grant, for all her high connections now, certainly came from nothing, but her continual relationship with those whom she knew before her family's elevation was a credit to her. So many people forget who they were once they become something better, in his opinion at least.

"Now, I think that is enough questions for Miss Grant. She's here to enjoy herself and not be hounded by you lot." His sister turned to Miss Grant. "If ye like, this afternoon my brother has to oversee some of the tenant farms here. Would ye like to join him?"

Her gaze snapped to his and with little choice thanks to his meddling sister, he said, "Ye're more than welcome, Miss Grant. It shoudna take too long and 'tis a nice enough day for a ride."

She studied him a moment, her teeth working her bottom lip as she decided what to do. Brice couldn't tear his gaze from her mouth and all thoughts filled his mind of how soft her lips may be.

"If you're sure," she said at length, her words uncertain.

Brice pushed up from his seat, striding toward the door. "'Tis fine, Miss Grant. I'll meet ye at the front foyer in an hour." Brice strode from the room, heading toward his own to change. He would have a word with his meddling sister who wanted him to act the host and tour guide it would seem. He wasn't laird for amusement's sake, he had work to do, people to attend. Running about the lands and showing a Sassenach his home wasn't one of them.

When he returned he would have a stern word with Elizabeth and ensure she kept her busybody self out of his business. And keep the delectable, sweet and alluring Miss Grant away from him also.

✦

An hour later, they met in the foyer and with very few words spoken, the laird made his way toward a large stone building near the rear of the house. The stables were a long, rectangular-shaped structure with multiple stalls, all of them filled with both working horses and pleasure mounts.

"Ye may ride Elizabeth's horse. She's a placid mare, and will no throw ye.'"

Sophie walked up to the stall he pointed to, crooning as

31

the mare made her way over to her and placed her soft velvety nose into Sophie's gloved palm. "What a sweetie you are," she said, leaning over and kissing her horse's nose.

"Can ye ride?" he asked, stopping to stare at her.

Sophie frowned, not liking his tone or the fact that just because they had been poor did not mean they could not ride a horse. Which, in truth, neither she nor Stephen could when Louise had first married the marquess, but Luke had put an end to that and taught them both very well.

"The marquess taught me. I'm sure I'll be able to keep up." She raised her brow at him and he turned his back to her, yelling out orders to a nearby stable hand to saddle her mount.

Sophie stepped back and kept out of everyone's way as they readied the horses. Her mare was a pretty brown and had the sweetest eyes. She glanced at the laird, watching as he busied himself with his horse, the corded muscles on his arms visible even under his shirt. He wasn't wearing his kilt today. Instead he was wearing a shirt, greatcoat, tan trews and boots.

Heat prickled her skin as her eyes took their fill of him. She'd never seen such a handsome man before, certainly in London the gentlemen whom Louise had introduced her to were nothing like this Scottish one.

The men in London seemed like boys compared to this man.

"Are ye ready, lass?"

She jumped at his curt question, meeting his gaze. One eyebrow was raised and she nodded, trying to ignore the fact that he'd caught her staring at his person.

"Of course." A stableman led her mare up to her and, using the mounting block beside the stall door, hoisted herself up into the leather saddle.

The laird didn't wait for her, simply pushed his horse into

a trot, leaving her to scramble behind to catch up. It was little use, as soon as his larger, more powerful mount made it outside, he pushed him into a canter and Sophie pulled up her mare, watching him.

What was he doing? Was he taking her for a ride to see some tenant farms or being a total ass and leaving her behind to get lost?

She pushed her mount into a walk. If he did not want her to come with him he only need say. Did the man have no manners? She rode for a few minutes on the grounds near the estate and never far enough that she could not see the house through the trees.

The sound of thumping hooves echoed in the woods and she continued on, wanting to ignore the Scottish buffoon since he found it so very easy to ignore her.

He appeared through the trees, his brow furrowed in a deep scowl. "What are ye doing, lass? Ye're supposed to be following me."

Sophie walked her mare over to his, stopping before him. "You took off so fast that I wasn't quick enough to see where you went. If you did not wish for me to accompany you, you only had to say. I would've been quite content to stay at the house."

He rubbed his jaw, the action bringing her attention to his mouth. Damn it, she didn't need to see how very lovely his mouth was, even when pulled into a disapproving frown.

"Ye said you could ride. Are ye a liar?"

Sophie sighed. "Oh no, I can ride, but I will not chase you like a little puppy. A gentleman would wait for his partner before taking off ahead of her as if the devil himself was on his heels."

He looked away from her, mumbling something she could not make out. Although the word *devil* and *was chasing him* she did hear. "I never said I was a gentleman." His eyes snapped to hers. She swallowed, his penetrating stare doing odd things to her belly.

"I have other obligations today other than the tenant farms. I dinna need to be held up by an Englishwoman who canna ride."

Sophie glared. How dare he? "I think I shall return to the house. I do not wish to intrude on your time and be a burden." She swallowed hard the lump in her throat at his rudeness. What was wrong with the man? That he didn't like her was obvious and the thought of staying another night under his roof wasn't to be borne.

He pointed into the trees. "The house is that way. Good day to ye, Miss Grant."

She didn't bother to reply, simply turned her horse back toward the house and left. On her return to the stables she spied her coachman. "Peter, any word on the wheel and when it will be ready? I do wish to leave here as soon as possible."

Her coachman doffed his cap. "Yes, Miss Grant. The wheel will be no more than five days away. We'll be on our way soon enough."

"Thank you," she said, starting back toward the house. She made her room, slumping onto her bed. Gretel came in, bustling toward her.

"What are you doing back so soon? I thought you were out on a ride with the laird?"

The reminder made her fist her hands and punch the bed on either side of her. "The man is an oaf. He left me behind and then tried to say that I couldn't ride and keep up." She sat up, staring at nothing in particular. "We cannot leave soon enough. I fear our appearance here at his house is not what he wished."

Gretel came and stood before her, taking her hand. "It'll be alright, Miss Sophie. You know that Miss Mackintosh welcomes you here, and so you are her guest. Just ignore the laird. Like you said," Gretel remarked, going over to the fire and throwing on a couple of peat logs on to burn. "We'll be gone soon and all of the time here will be quickly forgotten."

If only he were that easy to forget. With his striking profile, his muscular frame and a face that would make even Lord Byron jealous it would not be an easy feat. To ignore his barbs and not react, a trait she was known to do, would not be the easiest thing in the world.

Sophie had always gotten along well with most people, so for the laird to be so very prickly left her discombobulated. "I think I'm going to have to talk to the laird to ensure our stay here is not against his will. It's his home, after all. I would hate to intrude."

"I'm sure he'll be back from the tenant farms soon. He spends most of the afternoons in the study downstairs."

Sophie glanced at Gretel, who busied herself cleaning up her combs and brushes on her dressing table. "How do you know that about the laird?" Something akin to jealousy shot through her at the thought of her friend knowing more about the man than she did. Why it would bother her so? She had not one clue and she didn't want to delve into those particulars right at this moment.

"Oh, the housekeeper Mrs. Kenny said. Like clockwork apparently the laird arrives at his study and doesn't leave until late in the afternoon, just in time to prepare for dinner."

Relief flowed through her that Gretel wasn't watching his every move. She shuffled off the bed, disgusted at her own thoughts. Gretel may be her servant, but she was also her friend. "I'm going to go for a walk about the house. Explore a little. I shall not be long."

Sophie walked into the corridor and started toward the passageway that led to the staircase. The house was enormous and she couldn't help but wonder that when the laird's sister married and left, what he would do with all this space.

But then she supposed, he too would be married and possibly filling the rooms with children.

She strolled through the smaller drawing room and into a little antechamber that overlooked the front yard. The sound of horses' hooves pulled her gaze to the window and she watched as the laird jumped down from his mount, handing his horse to a waiting stableman.

His long, purposeful strides to the house kept her attention on him and heat pricked her skin at the sight. She lifted her gaze to look out over the grounds, vexed at her own stupidity.

She was attracted to him. That was what was wrong with her. Even with his coarseness and overpowering ways, there was something about him that drew her to him.

Sophie had not thought she was the type of woman who enjoyed rakes, but here she was...enjoying this one quite a lot. Or at least, enjoying the view of him, not so much when he opened his mouth.

Moving away from the window, she made her way through an upstairs sitting room, past a stairway that went up in the tower that sat central to the home. She passed another staircase leading downstairs and then came to a long passage. The walls were lined with family portraits and there was a long Aubusson runner that ran the length of the parquetry floor.

Sophie strolled slowly, looking at each of the family portraits of the laird's ancestors. All of them looked stern, but there was something about their eyes that was kind. The children always appeared happy and carefree and she couldn't help but wonder if any of them were of the current Laird Mackintosh.

At the end of the passage stood another window and

Sophie glanced outdoors, seeing that this vista was simply too perfect for words.

"What are ye doing in this part of the house?"

Sophie let out a little squeak at the stern question. She'd not heard him join her. She turned, glancing up at the highlander who embodied everything that every young debutante in London dreamed of.

Herself included. His hair was mussed from his ride, his clothing mud-splattered and damp, and she'd never seen a more handsome gentleman even when at the finest balls in London.

"I was looking around, my lord. I promise I won't steal anything," she said, a little more sternly than what was required. She pushed past him. She didn't have to stay in this part of the house. There were still many places left to explore, including the tower. The laird could keep his little secluded wing all to himself.

He clasped her arm and then dropped it just as quickly. "I dinna mean to offend ye, lass. But ye shouldn't be in this part of the house. 'Tis not seemly."

She scoffed at his use of the word as she tried to stifle a smile. "Seemly?" At the voicing of the word she chuckled. "I do apologize. I shall leave. I would hate for your reputation to be ruined."

"Are ye laughing at me?" he asked, stepping toward her.

The urge to flee rode hard on her heels, but she didn't move. Something told her that if she did he would follow close on her heels. Not an unwelcome thought, unfortunately. Maybe she ought to run.

"A little, but I promise my amusement is only limited to your words, not anything else."

"So ye dinna find me amusing? I thought after our morning that ye would think me nothing but an ass."

Sophie did chuckle then, taking a breath and relaxing a

little. "Oh, I did find you one of those, but if you show me about your tower I may forgive you your ungentlemanly manners."

He stared at her a moment, and his dark, hooded eyes that ran over her person sent a delicious shiver across her skin. Sophie fought not to fidget at his inspection of her. Instead she held his gaze, not willing to let him know just how very nervous he made her.

"Very well, I'll show ye the tower. Come," he said, striding past her and back toward the staircase. Sophie took in his back, her gaze sliding over his bottom. Trews really were lovely fitting pants for men.

She hastened after him, his steps long and quick, eating up the distance to where the tower door sat open. He made the entrance and she followed. The tower was of stone construction and smelled a little musty. Goosebumps pricked on her skin at the temperature change and she followed him up the stone stairs that were worn down by hundreds of years of footsteps.

"How amazing to know that your ancestors all walked these very rooms, each and every step that we walk on they too have placed their feet."

He nodded. "I know, it has always been a fascination with me too. The house is old, with many stories to tell."

"If only it would speak," she said, meeting his gaze.

He smiled, the first one she'd seen and the first one she had pulled forth. She sighed. How was the man more handsome than anyone she'd ever met before? And why did he have to live so very far away from her home in London? Far away from her family?

"Come, the view from the top is remarkable."

The view from where Sophie stood was pretty impressive as well, she mused.

CHAPTER 5

*B*rice counted each stone step leading up to the top of the tower. Anything to keep himself distracted from the woman who followed him.

Miss Grant was a diversion that he didn't need to endure right at the moment, not when he was on the cusp of offering marriage to Elspeth. A union between the Mackintosh and Brodie clans had been long desired—both their parents, may his rest in peace, had wanted the union. He could not ignore his father's last dying wish.

Determined to ignore the unearthly pull he had toward the lass, he turned his mind onto his responsibilities for tomorrow. He had planned to go hunting, possibly even stay out at the lodge for a night or two. The idea of being away from home no longer tempted him as much as it should.

He could guess as to why.

"Just a few more steps and we'll be at the top." He cast a glance over his shoulder and her eyes flicked up to meet his. His step faltered and he cursed himself a fool for not concentrating. He'd break his neck soon and then where would he be?

"I'm glad. I do not think that I've climbed up a tower this steep before or with this many steps. How many are there?"

"One hundred and eighty if ye're counting from the first floor up. The steepness of them makes it feel like there are more than there are."

She chuckled and his skin prickled. He liked the sound of her genuine, throaty laugh. He'd like to hear it more often.

"I suppose it would."

He came to a door at the top of the stairs and, pushing it, held it open for Miss Grant. She stepped past him, and he took the opportunity to admire her up close. He really needed to get a command on himself. She was not for him. She was for some London fop who lived in England and within an easy distance to her siblings. No English lass wanted to move to the highlands of Scotland. No sane one anyway.

The wind was strong this afternoon and a small smile played about his lips as he watched her battle with her hair and try to take in the view before them at the same time. It was a pointless exercise as the wind had already won this war.

Her golden locks whipped about her shoulders and face, giving her the air of country lass, without care or vanity. He liked what he saw.

"'Tis beautiful is it not?"

She glanced at him, nodding once. "It is the most beautiful country and I'm looking forward to seeing more of it."

He looked out over the grounds, forcing himself to glance away from Sophie. "I suppose ye're referring to yer friend ye're visiting in the highlands. Where does she reside?"

"Jean resides near the Isle of Skye. I've not been there before, but she writes that it has the most delightful walks if one enjoys the sea and forest."

"I've been to Skye. Ye'll enjoy yer time there if it's one of a recreational kind." To live there and earn a living from farming was not an easy occupation. The life was hard, fickle, and the seasons, harsher farther north, made farming difficult. "Is Miss Jean in service?"

She frowned, stepping up to the turret and looking out over the courtyard below. "She works as a tutor, but her mother has been ill and so she's been home for several months. Jean and I became friends at school in Sandbach." Sophie turned to him, smiling. "She reminds me of you actually."

He raised his brow, surprised at such a thing. "How so?" he found himself asking, wanting to know more about her and her life. And more importantly how a woman could be similar to him.

"First and foremost I suppose it's the Scottish burr and then the hair, although yours is a darker shade of red, more burnt copper, Jean has fiery-red locks." She stepped closer to him, reaching up to touch a strand, running it through her fingers.

He stared at her, having never been touched by a woman he hardly knew, at least in such a forward manner. Whether she knew what she was doing was improper or not, her touch caused his heart to beat loudly in his ears. There was little chance he'd remind her of her inappropriateness and have her move away.

An overwhelming urge to reach out and clasp her about her small waist and hoist her hard up against his body assailed him and he clamped his hands firmly at his sides. He would not allow temptation to sway him from what both the Mackintosh and Brodie clans desired. Elspeth would suit him well enough. Give him the bairns both families needed to ensure the family lines continued. Keep everyone happy.

All except for him...

He pushed the thought aside. He would be happy enough,

especially when he had a son or daughter. To hold his own bairns would make a marriage to a woman he respected and liked, but did not love, endurable.

She let go of his hair, dismissing him and walking toward the other side of the tower. "I've always been very jealous of people who have unusual hair colors. My hair is plain and common."

"There is nothing common about ye." The moment the words left his mouth he wanted to rip them back. And the delight that crossed her features at his words made him realize his mistake. He didn't need to flatter her. He only ever need be polite. She would never be anything to him. His fate was sealed. That her sister had married into nobility also sealed her fate to a point. Even if she did not know it, her sister would expect her to marry well. Into the London sphere in which they circulated and to a man of equal standing to that of the marquess. She would not want her sister to marry beneath her.

"Thank you, my lord. How very nice of you to say." She looked at him as if she could see his statement left him uneasy and found this amusing.

He gestured toward the view, wanting to change the subject. "If ye look here ye can see Loch Moy through the trees. We swim there when the weather permits."

"I've not swam in years," she said, her disappointed tone pulling at something behind his ribs. "Not since I was a child at least."

He didn't like the idea of her missing out on the simple things that made life worth living. Swimming, laughing, playing. All of those things that he'd adored as a child, and still partook in at times as an adult. "'Tis spring, mayhap we'll get a day while ye're here that'll permit me to take ye down to the loch."

"Really?" Her eyes brightened and she smiled. "I'd like that very much," she said as she continued to take in the view. "Although I have nothing to wear."

He cleared his throat, the imagery of her wearing very little or nothing at all while swimming tortured his mind. Miss Grant was a beautiful woman, with a body that would make Venus jealous. God save him, but a part of him had offered just so he could enjoy seeing her wet and at his mercy.

He was going to hell.

"Elizabeth has attire that will fit ye well enough, but as I said, we'll have to wait and see if the weather permits. It may be the case that ye'll be back to yer travels before we can go."

"That would be a shame." She glanced up at him, her dark-blue orbs glinting with mirth. "I should like to swim with you."

Heat prickled his skin and he turned abruptly, needing to move, to get away from the temptation that Miss Grant offered. Why she affected him so he could not understand. Perhaps it was because he could not have her. And damn it all to hell, he wanted her. Just one taste. One stolen moment would satisfy him for the many years that loomed before him. But alas, he knew that he could not act on his desires. He was destined for a marriage that would be as cold as a highland winter where there would be no swimming in spring or stolen kisses. Where there would be nothing at all except duty.

The following day Sophie smiled as Gretel handed her a swimming outfit that Elizabeth had loaned her. She strode to the window, throwing up the sash and feeling the temperature of the air. It was decidedly chill and she sighed, disappointed that today would not be the day the laird took her swimming.

She went about her morning routine, bathing and dressing in one of the new gowns Louise had purchased for her before traveling to Scotland.

The breakfast room was empty upon her arrival and she looked at the clock on the mantel. Had she slept in? "Has everyone breakfasted before me?" she asked as a footman set a plate of ham and toast before her, along with a cup of tea. She added a dash of milk.

"Miss Mackintosh and Miss Brodie have requested trays in their room this morning as the laird has traveled to Inverness for the day."

"Oh," was all she managed. The day was simply getting worse and worse.

Why she longed to see the laird again she could not fathom, not after how he'd treated her on the horse ride the other day. But in the tower yesterday she couldn't help but think she'd glimpsed a part of him he didn't often show, and she liked what she saw.

He wasn't so disapproving and cold. Quite the opposite. In fact, he seemed genuinely interested in her past and wanted to take her swimming.

The idea of being in the water with him, having him touch her, left her skin to prickle with expectation.

She shivered at the idea of his hands sliding over her flesh, of holding her in strong, capable hands. Sophie glanced out the window, willing the weather to be warmer tomorrow so she might feel exactly what she wanted.

Him.

She took a sip of tea, sighing at the sweet, rejuvenating tonic. She wanted to ensure that the truce that had sprouted between them continued, and the laird didn't revert back to the cold, cutting self he was the other day. He was much preferable this way, and with time perhaps he would tell her a little about himself, just as she had.

The day passed in a reasonable manner. After breakfast she'd gone to the library and picked out a book on the Scottish clans, wanting to know more about his people and the culture.

Sophie had then looked about the first floor, walking through the great hall that was a room stuck in a time past. With a great hearth at one end and the dais that sported six chairs before it at the other, she could imagine the lairds of old sitting before their subjects, eating hearty meals and listening to music and clan gossip.

Rows of tables sat within the hall. In years past the stone would've been covered in rushes, wolfhounds would have skulked about the clansmen's legs, men and women living under the patronage of the Mackintosh laird, eating and enjoying their time within the fold.

Sophie sat in a large, leather wingback chair set before a large bank of windows overlooking the grounds. She flicked through the book on clans, taking in the different tartans and the boundaries to each clan's lands.

"'Tis good to see ye taking an interest in the clans, lass." Brice leaned over her chair, pointing out the Mackintosh clan's land. "We've been here centuries and God willing we'll be here hundreds of years more."

"I've always found history interesting and Scottish history is full of clan wars, wars against England. Culloden comes to mind." She turned in the chair and met his gaze. "Did your clan suffer any losses at Culloden?"

"Aye," he said, a small frown marring his otherwise perfect brow. "Too many, but alas, 'tis a war the Scots were determined to have and so as with any war, good men are lost."

She turned back to the book, closing it. "I've been looking

about your house, learning all its different corridors and staircases. Did you know you have seven staircases throughout the house?"

He sat down across from her, grinning, and she couldn't look away from his disheveled auburn hair or the wicked amusement that glowed in his eyes. "Actually, we have ten, two are servants' staircases."

Sophie chuckled. "Ten? If two are servants' stairs, that makes nine. Where is the tenth staircase?"

"Oh aye, there is a dungeon staircase. Did ye not find that today on yer travels?"

The thought sent a shiver across her skin and she shook her head. "No, I did not, but it sounds fascinating." He didn't further elaborate and Sophie wondered if she should ask him to show her. A little forward some would say, but the idea of seeing a dungeon, something she'd never seen before was too much of a temptation to pass up.

"Will you show me?"

He stood, holding out his hand. Sophie took it, and the moment her hand touched his a shock of awareness ran up her arm. His hand was warm and large and she couldn't help but think of how those very capable hands could hold her close, keep her from harm. "Of course, I'll show ye."

*B*rice made their way down to the cellars, which led farther into the two dungeons the castle boasted. They were made during the construction of the house, but very little information remained on who was held there or why.

As a child he'd played down here often, never finding it scary, damp or ominous. Elizabeth on the other hand refused to come down here, stating the rooms were haunted by a dark-cloaked monk.

The small, narrow tunnel leading down to the dungeon was made of rough rock. An old rush lamp sat just where the cellar lights dissipated, and using flint, Brice lit the rush, bathing the area in light.

He bit back a smile when he felt Sophie clasp the back of his coat, holding him for support.

"Are ye alright, lass? Not afraid are ye?"

"My holding on to you is not obvious enough that I'm terrified?" She chuckled and her laugh, both self-deprecating and soft, did odd things to his body, made him feel things he shouldn't. Made him want things he couldn't have.

"There is nothing down here to be scared of. I promise ye that."

They came into the first of three chambers. Brice lifted the rush lamp and showed Sophie the walls. Even after the hundreds of years, they still sported chains and bolts hammered into the rock. The walls were damp, water oozing from the surface. "It would not have been the nicest place for people to be kept."

She stepped around him and looked about the space. She clasped her arms before her, rubbing them. "It's cold in here. Do you not feel like someone is watching us?"

Brice shrugged, glancing about also, anything to keep him from staring at the sweet Sassenach before him. "I dinna feel anything, but Elizabeth refuses to come down here too, so mayhap there are spirits still lingering, waiting to be freed."

Right at that moment, the rush lamp blew out and darkness enfolded them. Brice stood there a moment, the hair on the back of his nape standing upright. No such thing had ever occurred before. He gasped as Sophie threw herself against him, her arms holding his waist in an unyielding grip, her head huddled against his chest.

He wrapped his arms about her and turned her toward where he knew the tunnel entrance was. "I'll take ye back upstairs," he said, her muffled reply unintelligible against his chest.

He held her tight, probably closer than he needed to, but he liked the way she felt in his arms. Holding out his hand he came to the wall and worked his way across until he felt the tunnel entrance. They walked slowly and Brice kept his hand above him to ensure he didn't let a low, overhanging rock hit him or Sophie.

"I do not think I'll come back down here again," she said, just as the light from the cellar started to penetrate the space.

Brice had to admit to feeling a little relief at making it back. He'd never had a candle or the rush lamp go out on him just as it did back then, and even he could admit to feeling a little unsettled by it.

"'Tis all well now, Miss Grant. I'll not let any harm come to ye."

She pulled him to a stop, glancing up at him. Unable to keep his attention anywhere but on the woman in his arms he met her gaze.

His stomach clenched as she studied him, her face still a little ashen from her fright. He pushed a lock of hair away from her face, slipping it behind her ear.

An overwhelming need assailed him to pull her close, lean down and kiss those delectable lips that were slightly apart and plump, ripe for the picking.

"Here ye are, I've been looking all over the house for ye."

Sophie wrenched out of his arms and inwardly cursed the arrival of his sister. Elizabeth had an uncanny ability to turn up at the least unwelcome times.

"I was showing Miss Grant the dungeons. We lost our lighting and I was assisting Miss Grant toward the light."

What on earth was he saying? He shut his mouth with a snap before anything else absurd came spilling out.

"Really?" His sister glanced between them and he recognized that stare well. She was summing him up, wondering what really was going on.

He clasped his hands behind his back lest he wrench Miss Grant back beside him. He'd wanted to kiss her, had been seconds away of doing exactly that. Perhaps he ought to thank his sister for interrupting them when she did. There was something about Miss Grant that made Brice realize that one taste of her would never be enough.

"We've served tea in the drawing room upstairs. Come, Sophie, we'll walk up together. Elspeth will join us there."

Brice watched them go, waiting a few minutes before he followed them up the cellar stairs. What had he been thinking? The reminder that Elspeth waited for his proposal sent shame spiraling through his blood.

He owed it to his parents to fulfill their most-cherished wish. God knows he'd been difficult enough with all other things in his life while they were alive. He at least ought to do this one thing for them, even though it was too late to make amends for being a difficult child.

Brice made for the library, wanting solitude and time to think. He needed a plan that would keep his hands off Miss Grant while also gaining enough courage to ask Elspeth for her hand in marriage.

Neither option was appealing. He shut the library door and made his way over to his decanter of whiskey instead. A drink first, then everything else that he was to do would come next.

CHAPTER 6

Sophie watched the laird during dinner that evening, wondering if she'd imagined that he was going to kiss her earlier today. He'd certainly had a wolfish look about him as he leaned toward her before his sister interrupted them.

All afternoon she'd been edgy, annoyed and fidgety that they had been interrupted. That in itself was vexing as the laird had not been the kindest to her when she'd first arrived here, but perhaps it was just his way. The day they were to go riding he'd been busy and she had been thrown into his care.

Whereas today he'd offered to take her down to the dungeons. He'd had spare time to spend with her. His property was vast, it was possible that his coldness toward her the other day had been simply because he'd not had time to mind her.

She shivered as she remembered his hands, clasping her firmly about the waist, holding her fast before him. It had taken all her willpower not to lean into his touch when he'd placed her hair behind her ear.

She swallowed, reaching out to take a sip of wine. She

glanced at him and found him watching her. His gaze took in her face and dipped over her body and Sophie's breath caught in her lungs. With each inspection over her person she swore she could feel it as if he were touching her himself.

She'd had men look at her so in London, certainly after her sister had married the marquess and placed her higher in society. That her brother-in-law had bestowed on both her and her brother a modest inheritance also helped.

But with the way the Laird of Mackintosh drank her in, as if she were the sweetest honey to swallow, a thrumming ache formed low in her belly and she couldn't help but wonder what it would be like to be taken in his arms, kissed within an inch of her life.

How delectable that would be.

Her skin heated, but she would not look away from him. If he were trying to scare her away, or warn her off with his heated gaze, he'd mistaken her character for a woman who could not hold her own. She was a Grant, not a woman to be toyed with or assumed to be weak simply because she was female. If he would look at her so boldly, then she would in turn take her fill and take a portrait of him in her mind for the many years to come when hundreds of miles separated them and they went on with their busy lives.

Elizabeth cleared her throat and only then did his lordship look away.

"I was thinking since the weather has been so lovely that we may picnic at the Viking ruins tomorrow. Would ye like that, Sophie?"

To visit Viking ruins sounded simply wonderful and she nodded. "I would love to see them. I understand that the Scots have a lot of ancestry to thank the Vikings for."

Elizabeth smiled, spooning some soup into her mouth. "We do. If ye have not noticed my brother is obscenely tall and walks about as if he should have a sword in his hand."

Sophie chuckled and his lordship scoffed. "Who says I dinna have a sword, sister?"

The idea of seeing him wield one was not an image she needed to imagine. She was already picturing him too perfectly as it was. Even so, to explore outside the house, see a little of the Scotland she wanted to before their carriage broke down sounded like a wonderful day out.

♛

*T*he carriage ride to the ruins was of short duration and it wasn't long before servants set up a small table and chairs along with food and wine.

The ruins were located in a heavily wooded area near a small river that apparently ran into Loch Moy. "The Vikings would use waterways to transport their goods, and travel."

She glanced up at the laird, having not heard him come up behind her. His voice ran over her like a soothing balm and she couldn't think of a more pleasant way to pass the time than to listen to his Scottish brogue.

"Will you show me about?"

He glanced toward where Elspeth and Elizabeth sat at the table, having tea and biscuits. "Aye, of course. This way." He gestured for her to precede him and she went ahead.

They walked on in silence for a time before his lordship said, "I must admit that I've never met a woman like ye, Miss Grant. Ye're not what I expected when ye arrived at Moy castle."

"Really?" she asked, curious to know what he thought of her. "What did you think I'd be like?"

"Spoiled. A London debutante who was used to getting her own way and would look down on anyone she deemed beneath her."

Sophie raised her brow, halting her steps. "You do not

have a very high opinion of the English, then." She continued on and felt more than heard that he was close on her heels. "I suppose because I'm not spoiled and have known menial chores in my life that I'm not like that. Not that I do not enjoy having servants now, I must admit I loathed having to wash my own clothes, but no, I would never look down on anyone for their situation in life. I know my future would have been vastly different had my sister not married a marquess."

"I'm very glad that yer sister did marry the marquess."

Again she stopped and turned to face him, settling her gaze on his. They were hidden from view here within the trees. Through the foliage about them she could make out the stone ruins of the Viking location. "Why do you say that?"

Their eyes met and held. Her heart beat like a drum in her ears, and if she were of a more delicate constitution her knees may have given out on her in that moment. He was devilishly handsome and oh so tempting.

"We would not have met had she not."

She smiled, pleased he would think such a thing and say it aloud to her. "We may have still met, but I doubt your sister would've invited me to stay." A sad truth when one was beneath another due to wealth and rank. How many people missed marrying their soul mate due to being married off to other people that family and society thought appropriate?

She would never do such a thing. If she fell in love with an innkeeper or farmer she would marry him and enjoy her life and love. She would even leave London and her family if it meant living with the man who made her heart flutter. Even if that meant leaving her family whom she'd only just been reunited with after all the years apart.

"If she had not invited ye, I would have I'm sure."

She raised her brow. "Really? You did not seem too fond

of me accompanying you the other day horse riding. Are you certain you would've invited me to stay?"

He ran a hand over his jaw, looking up at the sky as if it would help him explain himself that day before looking at her. "I apologize for leaving ye behind and being so rude." He frowned and she wondered what was going through his mind. "I acted appallingly and I hope ye forgive me."

"I will think about it," she said, turning toward the ruins. Her booted foot caught a stick and Sophie toppled forward, the ground coming up fast to meet her nose. Strong, capable arms wrapped about her waist and stopped her fall.

He wrenched her back against his chest and she sighed, the hardness of him against her back warmed places in her body no lady should know could be warmed.

She turned in his arms, determined to thank him and move away but her feet wouldn't budge from their spot. Her blood pumped loud and fast in her ears and she watched, enthralled, as he leaned down and, finally, kissed her.

His mouth covered hers and her mind whirred at the softness of his lips. For a man who was all brawn and muscle, hard about the edges, his lips were soft, supple and sending her wits to spiral.

Sophie leaned up on her tiptoes and kissed him back, not willing to miss out on such a situation in life that had never been afforded to her before.

His hands tightened about her waist, slid about her back and pulled her close. Her nipples ached and through her thin muslin gown she prayed he could not feel what he was doing to her body. He broke the kiss, staring at her as if she'd grown two heads.

"I suppose this is where you tell me you're sorry for kissing me and that it won't happen again," she said, breathless.

His lips twitched. "Nay, lass. This is where I tell ye that now that I've tasted yer sweet lips, I'll be doing it again."

👑

*B*rice took her lips again, heedless of who may come upon them. At this point he did not care who saw them kissing. He liked the lass, she was kind, intelligent and unlike anyone he'd ever known. Certainly he'd never met a Sassenach like her.

He pulled her close, her warmth and scent of lilies intoxicating his senses and making his head spin. Her kiss, untutored at first, followed his lead and he edged his tongue slowly into her mouth, inwardly crowing when she made a delectable mewling sound of pleasure.

"Ye're so sweet, lass," he said between kisses, holding her close and dipping his head yet again. She met his desire for her with that of her own and he growled when she tentatively pressed her tongue to his.

"Yes, lass, that's it." He wanted her to try, to tempt and tease him as much as he was trying to tempt her. It had been so long since he'd wanted a woman in such a way. Certainly a good few months since he'd bedded a lass. Such a courtship was a night of pleasure and little else. A woman who understood he wasn't looking for a wife any more than she was looking for a husband.

But the lass in his arms now, untouched and perfect in so many ways, was not for him. The reminder ought to have made him wrench away, apologize and leave her just as she'd said earlier, but he didn't. If anything it made him want to take all and everything she offered him. To be with her as long as she would stay at Moy.

She pulled back, breaking the kiss and immediately he missed having her in his arms. Sophie stared up at him with something akin to awe and he knew deep down, to part from her, have her leave when her carriage was repaired, would be hard.

Hard to watch and hard to allow.

Her hand fluttered up to touch her lips, now red and a little swollen from his touch. "I've never been kissed like that before."

Damn it all to Hades, he'd never kissed anyone like that before either. Certainly not with the simmering emotion he felt coursing through his veins. He liked this lass and that in itself was more telling than anything. To spend more time with her would only mean he'd become more attached, less likely to let her go.

He could not walk that path, no matter how tempting it was to go against everything he'd promised his parents. Elspeth was to be his wife. Not an English lass that, due to no fault of her own, ended up in his town.

"Did ye like my kiss?" he couldn't help but ask. He was a glutton for punishment.

She nodded, her eyes glazed in wonder. "I did." She stepped against him, taking his hand. "While I do not know what such a kiss means, if anything or nothing, I will tell you this. While I'm here at Moy, and a guest in your home, if you feel the inclination to kiss me in such a way again, I'm more than open to it."

He chuckled, unable not to. "'Tis a fine idea, lass. I'm in agreement of yer proposal."

"Very good. Now, shall you show me the ruins?"

"Come," he said, leading them toward the old fort. "There is much to see."

$\mathcal{S}$ophie found herself staring at the laird on and off during the remainder of the day. Within a few minutes of stepping into the old Viking ruins, they were joined by Elizabeth and Elspeth, who both had childhood stories of playing within the grounds, of fascinating finds, like swords and coins, along with what they thought the different buildings and areas that spread out through the wooded area were used for.

The day was long but enjoyable, and Sophie had to admit that she felt quite at home here so far north in Scotland and so very far away from her family.

While she tried to take everything in about the ancient site, her mind kept wandering to the kiss she'd shared with the laird. What did it mean? Was he going to start courting her? Did he see her as a possible candidate for a wife?

She had very little experience with such matters. Her life in Sandbach had been closeted, her aunt venturing out very little unless it had something to do with their church.

When she had left Cheshire for London and to live with Louise, although she'd stepped out in Society at times, nothing like what just occurred with the laird had ever happened to her in Town.

If he did wish to marry her, make her his wife, Moy was a very long way from her family and she'd only just gotten them back. They had been separated from Louise since their older sister was only eight years of age. Sophie wasn't sure she was ready to part from her yet, or certainly part from her when the Scottish highlands were so very far away.

She sat at the small table set up for their luncheon and dismissed the fanciful thoughts. The laird had simply kissed her. To read anything more into the act would be silly and she would be foolish to believe that from one kiss one could decide to spend the rest of their lives with that person.

She was sure there were plenty of people in London who kissed and did not expect a marriage proposal the very next day.

"What do you think of the lemon pie, Sophie?" Elizabeth asked, biting into her own portion.

Sophie glanced down at her plate, having forgotten the food sitting untouched before her. She forked a piece of the pie and placed it in her mouth. "It's very good," she said, between chews.

Laughter caught her attention and she looked over to where the laird was walking with Elspeth. Elspeth was laughing at something the laird had said, and she was smiling up at him. It was the first time she'd seen Elspeth react in any way toward the laird. Sometimes when his lordship tried to engage her in conversation, Elspeth looked bored and disinterested at best. "Elspeth looks very pretty today," Sophie said, watching the two and ignoring the bite of jealousy that assailed her.

Elizabeth looked to where her brother was walking. "Yes, she does. We've been friends since infancy and our parents were the best of friends."

"She's spent a great deal of time here from what she said earlier." Sophie did not understand why she needed to know these things, but something inside her chilled at the sight of the laird with another woman. A Scottish, eligible woman.

"We all grew up together practically, either here or Elspeth's home Brodie Hall."

She watched as the couple walked, arms linked, toward the river that ran past where they were picnicking. "And Elspeth has not married?"

Elizabeth popped a piece of fruit into her mouth and shook her head. "Nay, she's never been inclined as far as I know. Although an heiress and set to inherit her father's holdings, she'd be a catch for anyone."

Even the Laird Mackintosh...

The words were unspoken, but they hung in the air all the same. A warning of sorts assailed her that perhaps the laird wasn't looking at her for a wife at all, but the Scottish lass he'd grown up with and already cared for.

Sophie turned in her chair and glanced in a different direction, not wanting to think such a thing. The laird wouldn't kiss her and be setting his cap for someone else. He wouldn't do that. Scottish or English, he was a gentleman and to court two women at once would not be gentlemanly behavior.

The thought was little comfort for she knew very well that gentlemen did such a thing all the time and she'd be a simpleton indeed to think this one was any different.

CHAPTER 7

*L*ater that night Sophie sat at the desk in her room and penned a letter to Louise. She had never been one not to be honest and open and so she told her sister of her growing feelings for the laird Mackintosh.

She threw her quill down on the desk, a sense of impatience overcoming her. Sophie looked out the window and stared at her reflection instead of the outdoors, the daylight giving way to night. The house had been abed for hours, even her maid Gretel was long asleep, but it eluded Sophie. Her mind would not settle after her kiss this afternoon or the laird's marked attention toward Elspeth not long after.

She picked up her glass of water and found it empty. Her stomach rumbled and she sighed. There was no use in trying to sleep unless she had a little bite to eat and drink.

Sophie wrapped a shawl about her shoulders and, picking up a candle from atop the mantel, she made her way to the door and the servants' stairs that came out near the kitchen on the first floor.

She made the kitchen with little trouble, and with the

stove still simmering with coals, the room was warm and smelled of flour and baked meat. She walked along the table, lifting up some linens to see what food lay beneath and found some bread from dinner that evening.

She sat on a stool, pulled the plate toward her, and started to eat. The aroma of yeast filled her senses and she sighed in pleasure as her stomach stopped protesting its hunger.

"Are ye alright, Miss Grant? I was making my way upstairs when I saw ye come out of the servants' stairs."

Sophie jumped at the sound of the laird's voice and she chewed quickly, needing to swallow before she spoke. "I hope you do not mind me coming in here at this late hour. I was writing a letter to my sister and I found myself a little hungry."

He came into the room, wearing nothing but trews and a shirt, which scandalously was not tucked into his pants. There was no cravat, a smooth, tanned chest peeked out from his untied top and his hair looked mussed as if he'd run his hand through it too many times.

Her stomach clenched, all hunger deserted her for another hunger altogether. She stared at him, taking her fill and not quite believing that he'd kissed her. After their little slip in etiquette, he'd kept a polite distance for the remainder of the afternoon, never cold or aloof, but he was certainly watchful for what he said or did.

But now, here in the small, warm room, her body longed to be in his arms again and she couldn't help but hope that he wanted to kiss her again too.

"Ye are more than welcome to whatever ye want, whenever ye want, lass." He walked over to a nearby cupboard and pulled out a bottle of wine. "Cook always keeps a well-aged red in here. I'll have a drink with ye and then escort ye back upstairs."

Sophie smiled, watching as he sat down opposite her across the table. He poured two glasses, sliding her drink across to her. She picked it up and drank deeply, parched after eating the bread and taking her fill of him.

"The bread is good, is it not? 'Tis one of my favorite dishes on a cold winter's night."

"It's very filling and fresh."

He reached over and she started as he wiped off what she imagined was a little crumb from her cheek. Her heart thumped loudly in her ears when he didn't immediately move away, and instead cupped her cheek in his hand.

"Ye're so beautiful, lass. I dinna know how I'm going to stay away from ye."

Sophie swallowed, having never heard such a sweet thing in her life. She stood and moved about the table to come to stand before him. He turned in his chair to face her and she reached up, smoothing out the small line that marred his forehead.

"You're not what I expected to find in the highlands either. You're quite a surprise, Laird Mackintosh."

He reached up and hugged her loosely about her back. "Call me Brice, please. I think after this afternoon we're past formal forms of address."

Her face heated a little at his reminder of what they'd done. "Will you call me Sophie?"

His mouth lifted in a small grin and her nerves skittered across her skin. "Aye. Sophie," he said, in a heavy brogue. "I can call ye that."

"I like the sound of my name on your lips," she whispered, stepping between his legs and coming up hard against him. His arms tightened about her back, his large hands splaying across her spine. It felt right. That she was in the right place for the first time in her life.

"I like the sound of yer name on my lips as well," he said, before he leaned up and kissed her.

Sophie met him halfway, having wanted to kiss him since the afternoon. The moment their lips touched, the agitation, the restlessness that had plagued her the whole night dissipated and everything was right in the world.

The kiss was everything and more. His mouth coaxed and tempted her, made her feel things she'd not known were possible between two people. His lips were soft, moved over hers like silk, his tongue tempting and warm against her own.

She met his kiss with her own, wanting to show him she too could tease and explore. His hand slid up her spine, sending a delicious shiver to course across her skin before he clasped her nape, turning her slightly to deepen the kiss.

Sophie clutched about his neck for purchase as the kiss turned from sweet and slow to something completely opposite. No longer did he tease and tempt her, the kiss now took on a life of its own. He kissed her hard, deepening the embrace and taking control of where the kiss was going.

Sophie's knees gave way and his arm clasped tight about her back, hoisting her onto his lap. She went willingly. How could she not? To be kissed in such a way made her mind blank, and she didn't wish to be good. Not right now in any case. She'd been well-behaved all her life. One scandalous kiss in a kitchen in the middle of the night would not hurt.

She didn't know when she'd get another opportunity for such a treat. Maybe with her husband if she was fortunate enough to marry a man like the laird who made her burn, made her mind constantly busy with thoughts of him.

"You're so sweet, lass. Ye make my teeth ache."

She pulled back, running a hand across his stubbled jaw. "Mine too," she said, seeing no reason not to be honest. He did make her long for more stolen kisses, for nights such as these that would never end.

Even if that meant that her time in England with her family, a family that had only recently been reunited, would be separated again by hundreds of miles.

He kissed her again, slower this time before he pulled back and helped her to stand. "I'll escort ye back to yer room. 'Tis late and the house can sometimes be hard to move through when the candles have all been doused."

Sophie checked that her dressing gown and shawl were still covering her before she allowed him to escort her from the room.

He took her hand, his large palm encasing hers as he led her from the kitchen. How was it that a simple touch of hands could discombobulate her so?

She glanced up at his profile, strong and rugged, a perfectly straight nose and cutting cheekbones. A devastatingly handsome man and one who made her stomach clench. Would he ever lose control with her? Would there be more kisses? Oh, how she hoped there would be.

Tonight, however, was not the night. The gentleman that he was, he escorted her to her room and simply bowed before leaving her staring after him. She watched as he strode back up the corridor, heading toward his own part of the house.

She sighed. "I hope I find a husband like you," she whispered into the dark. To live a life beside a man that excited, challenged and tempted her were what dreams were made of. Her sister had been so fortunate, maybe she would be as well.

In London no one had ever tempted her as much as Brice did, but that did not mean they were not out there. She simply needed to give it more time.

"Are you coming in, Miss Sophie?" Gretel asked, from inside the room.

"Oh yes, thank you," Sophie said, pulling off her shawl as she came inside and set it down on a nearby settee.

"Was that Laird Mackintosh I saw leaving down the hall?" Gretel asked, picking up the shawl and placing it over the back of a nearby chair.

Sophie went over to her bed, climbing in under the covers. "I went to the kitchens for some food. I'm sorry that I woke you. You may go back to bed now."

"May I speak plainly?" Gretel asked, standing at the end of Sophie's bed and ignoring Sophie's vague answer.

Sophie didn't like the sound of such a thing, but they had been friends for so long that she would not deny Gretel her opinion. Whatever it may be. Some women of nobility would never allow a maid to speak such, but that was not who Sophie was, or who she wanted to be. "If you like."

Gretel nodded. "Take care with the laird, miss. The staff here seem adamant that his lordship will marry the Scottish lass Elspeth and before the year is out. If that is the case, please take care if he happens to escort you back to your room in future."

Elspeth. Sophie frowned, having wondered the same thing, but having never heard this desire spoken aloud by anyone. "I'm sure you're mistaken," she said, her voice unsure even to her own ears. She played with her blankets, smoothing them out over her legs. "He's not injured me in any way, but should he be engaged to someone else, I'm sure he would be honest and tell me. We're friends, you see, and I can promise you the laird is not a deceiving man."

Gretel took in her words before moving back over to where the door to her adjoining room stood. "Even so, guard your heart. I do not wish to see you hurt. One never knows what the future holds."

"Goodnight, Gretel," Sophie said, putting an end to the conversation. The laird would not deceive her so. If he was intended elsewhere he would not kiss her with such passion. He would not kiss her at all.

She smiled at the memory of their interlude only minutes before and fell asleep dreaming of when she could do it again.

CHAPTER 8

The following morning Sophie came downstairs and found her driver kicking his heels in the foyer. "Good morning, Peter. Are you after me for something?" she asked, coming to stand before him.

"Miss Sophie, good morning. Yes, the wheel for the carriage arrived yesterday from Inverness and has been repaired. We can continue with our journey tomorrow if you wish."

Footsteps sounded on the parquetry floor and she turned to see Brice striding purposefully toward her. She bit her lip, and blinked at his kilt and shirt, his only articles of clothing. Heat rushed to her cheeks and she turned back to Peter only to see him contemplating her and the laird.

"Is there something the matter, lass?" Brice asked, coming to a stop beside her.

She shook her head. "No, nothing." She glanced up at him, her stomach summersaulting at being near him again. Her fingers itched to reach out and wrap about his waist, pull him close so he may kiss her again.

Sophie shook her head, dismissing the fanciful thought. She really did need to get a hold of her emotions.

"My carriage is repaired. Peter was just saying we may continue on with our journey tomorrow."

His smile slipped before he schooled his features. "We shall send word this afternoon regarding Miss Grant's travel arrangements." Brice clasped her hand and pulled her toward his study. "If ye'll excuse us."

Sophie didn't have the opportunity to say thank you to her servant before she was whisked into the laird's office where the door was shut, the snip of the lock loud in the empty, sizeable room.

"What are you doing, Brice? With the way you just acted, I'm not sure what my driver will think."

He walked over and then leaned up against his desk, watching her, his dark, hooded gaze pinning her on the spot. She fought not to fidget, although why she felt as if she were about to be scolded she had no idea.

"I dinna care what yer driver may think or anyone else. What I wish to know is if ye are going to be leaving me tomorrow?"

Leaving me? Sophie came up to him and uncrossed his arms covering his chest, placing them about her back. "Are we welcome to stay for a few more days then, my lord?"

He threw her a half smile, his grip about her waist increasing and making her belly clench. "Aye, ye're more than welcome. If fact, I'd love for ye to be a guest here for some weeks. Mayhap write to yer friend in the highlands and ask her to travel here to see ye. She'd be more than welcome also."

"Really? You'd do that for me?"

He leaned forward, brushing her lips with his. "Aye, I'd do that and more if it meant that I could keep ye here for a little while longer."

Sophie would love to have her friend come and stay and she would write her today and ask if she'd come. "I will ask her to stay, although I'm not certain she'll be able to. She helps her parents with the family income, but I will ask in any case."

He let her go and walked over to the fire and threw a log into the grate, watching the flames lick the wood. Sophie stayed where she was, unsure what was going through Brice's mind.

"Is everything well, Brice?"

He glanced at her and she wondered if it was regret that she glimpsed in his eyes. "'Tis a sweet sound hearing my name on yer lips, lass. Yes," he said, turning to face her. "All is well. The fact that yer carriage is ready has me wondering when ye will be leaving these parts. To continue on with yer travels either to the highlands or back to London."

Sophie came over near Brice and sat on a settee. "If Jean comes here, then after her stay I'll return to London. I received a letter only yesterday from Louise and she and Stephen miss me dreadfully, or so she says."

"Ye are close with yer siblings then?"

"Even though we were separated for many years, or at least Stephen and I were from Louise, we've always tried to stay close. Now that I have Louise back in my life, I do find I miss her dreadfully as well. I'm not ashamed to admit that I cannot wait to see them again."

He ran a hand over his jaw before that same hand ran through his hair, leaving it on end. "So our time with ye is limited. 'Tis a sad day that we'll have to bid ye farewell from our land."

"Even a Sassenach?" she teased, grinning.

He chuckled, coming to sit beside her, pulling her into the crook of his arm. "Aye, even an English lass such as yerself."

Some hours later Brice sat at his desk and went over the ledgers from his steward, yet his mind refused to concentrate. His thoughts kept straying to Sophie, who right at this moment was somewhere in his house, somewhere he was not.

His every waking hour he wanted to be near her, watch and admire how her pretty little hips shifted with each step. How her long, blonde locks caught the highland sun and glistened like ripe wheat.

The idea that her time here was limited left a hollowness inside. He wasn't fool enough to not know that he did not want her to go anywhere. Yet he could not ask her to stay either.

His path in life was set many years ago and Elspeth and her family were expecting a proposal in the coming months. He could not let them down, even if Elspeth seemed far from inclined to have him as her husband.

The lass had many times stated her desire to remain a spinster and had he not promised his parents he'd marry the lass, he'd be loath to disappoint Elspeth and take away her dream.

A knock at his door startled him from his reflections and he yelled *enter* more abruptly than was probably necessary.

His good friend Angus Campbell glanced about the threshold, smiling. "Brice, how are ye, my friend? 'Tis been an age since I've seen ye darken my threshold. I thought I'd come and darken yers instead."

Brice stood, gesturing him to enter. "Angus, 'tis good to see ye. More than ye know. Come," he said, walking about the desk to pour two whiskeys. "Sit and have a drink with me. I'm in need of advice."

Angus glanced at him as if he'd lost his mind, which Brice was starting to think he had. "Is something wrong? 'Tis not like ye to ask for help."

That was true, he very rarely asked for anything and yet, right now, Angus was the only person he could trust and confide in. He was his friend of many years, and both held confidences for the other that would never be told. Angus would listen and help steer him through this obstacle course called Sophie Grant.

He handed Angus a whiskey and sat back down. "What brings ye to these parts in any case? Ye're a long way from home."

"Aye." Angus nodded, taking a sip. "My sister has had a bairn and I'm on my way to see them at Avoch. If ye remember she married a landowner up there two years past."

"I remember it well. 'Twas a grand celebration that night. I'm glad yer sister is happily settled. How is Aberdeen?"

"The same." Angus studied him a moment before he said, "But I can see ye have something on yer mind. Out with it, man."

Brice sighed, leaning back in his chair, running a hand over his face. He'd never asked for such advice before and to do so now was out of character and foreign to him. "I dinna know what to do about a lass."

Angus raised his brow. "Are ye feeling well? Never would I ever thought to hear those words uttered from a Mackintosh's mouth."

Brice stared up at the ceiling in the hope that it may give him some divine insight into what he should do. "There is a woman here. Staying as a guest of my sister's. 'Tis a long story, but she came to stay after injuring herself in town. She's bonny."

A slow smile formed on Angus's lips. "How bonny?"

"She's the bonniest lass I've ever met and my troubles have now doubled because I canna keep my hands off her."

Angus did chuckle then, smiling fully. "Have ye tupped her?"

"Nay, she's the Marquess Graham's sister-in-law. To tup her would mean I'd have to marry her and ye know that I'm all but promised to Elspeth."

Angus rolled his eyes. "No matter what ye promised yer parents, or hers for that matter, I'll be surprised if Elspeth marries anyone. I've always thought she found men quite the bore, whereas women she seems more than happy to be around."

Brice narrowed his eyes, having never really taken much notice how Elspeth behaved around men, but now that his friend mentioned it, she did seem more inclined to converse with the female sex. Maybe she did not like men at all.

"'Tis not just my parents who expected a match. Elspeth's parents do too, and ye know they still believe we owe them our land due to that blasted loan Father took out from them before I was born. If everyone who wished for such a union were no longer living I wouldn't worry so much about the promise, but they are. I'd be letting them down if I dinna align the Mackintosh and Brodie clans together."

"That, my friend, is a load of horse dung. Elspeth's parents may long for whatever they like, but the debt has been paid, and why would ye not want yer daughter to marry with affection? Ye dinna have to do what anyone says. Ye're a Mackintosh, a laird. Ye may marry whomever ye want."

"A Mackintosh never goes back on their word, and I gave my word to my parents."

His friend threw him a consoling look before he said, "I understand, I do, but marriage is a lifelong commitment. Ye dinna want to be stuck with the wrong lass forever and a day. Marriage is nae supposed to be an endless cycle of torture."

Brice chuckled, glad of his friend's arrival and his words of wisdom, which all made sense, but still, he would need to think on what to do. He'd never broken his word to anyone before and to start doing so now for a woman that in all reality he hardly knew was foolish. In the coming weeks he would see how things went, and then make a decision at the end of it.

"Tell me ye are staying. We'll be having dinner soon. I'd love for ye to meet my guest."

Angus finished off his drink, placing the crystal glass down on his desk. "Now that I know of yer struggles ye'll not be getting rid of me, not for one night at least. I need to meet this English lass of yers and see what all the fuss is about."

Relief poured through him like a balm that his friend would be here, tonight at least, to support him. "Ye'll like her, Angus and then ye will be as confused as I am."

"Probably," his friend said, finishing his drink. "Now, where am I sleeping? I need to change before dinner."

👑

*A*t dinner that evening Brice sat at the head of the table and watched with growing annoyance as Angus and Sophie chatted to one another.

His sister had placed them together, and even though Brice trusted his friend with his life and everything else, the sight of him laughing, engaged, and enjoying the evening with his lass left a sour taste in his mouth.

He pushed about the roast potatoes on his plate, glancing up every now and then to see that they still spoke about all subjects, some of which even he had not discussed yet with her.

Elspeth on the other hand was reading some book that she tried to conceal under a napkin. Elizabeth, like him,

73

looked a little put out by Angus talking to Sophie and he narrowed his eyes, wondering if his sister held some feelings toward his friend.

Angus would be a good match for his sister and he knew him well enough to know that he would treat his sibling well. But knowing his friend as well as he did, he did not expect him to marry for some time yet. He enjoyed his bachelorhood too much.

He took a sip of wine, nodding to a waiting footman that the sweet course could be served. The pudding that was placed before him did little to lift his mood, even if it was one of his favorite dishes.

Sophie thanked the servant and glanced up the table toward him and a right hook to his stomach would've had less impact.

Her lips lifted into a knowing smile and he could not look away. The urge to go to her, wrap her up in his arms and kiss her to distraction overwhelmed him and he shook himself to remind himself they were in public.

There would be nothing of the sort, not unless she sought him out again or he came across her somewhere in the house when she was alone. It was one major advantage of having a house like this. One could get lost or remain lost so no one could interrupt or intrude on one's day.

He winked at her and smiled as a deep flush rose on her cheeks, making her even more beautiful to look at. His sister's clearing of her throat brought his attention to her and her pointed stare and raised brow was proof enough she'd caught him.

Brice turned back to his meal, eating his pudding with more zest than was necessary. There was nothing so bad that he'd done other than kiss the lass. Nothing wrong with him teasing her a little at the dining table either, even if his sister seemed overly shocked by his actions.

Who was he kidding? He was skating on thin ice and playing with fire at the same time. And yet, he could not remember a time when he'd enjoyed fire and ice so much in his life.

CHAPTER 9

The following day dawned warm and without a gust of wind to mar the beautiful spring weather. Yesterday after dinner Sophie had written to her friend Jean, inviting her to come and stay, and she hoped more than expected her to come. They were a family who worked for their living and times could sometimes be hard. A sojourn south to simply do nothing other than visit friends was not usual for them and so she didn't think she would be able to come.

Sophie sat outside on the lawn that her room overlooked. The grounds were vast and from here she could see down into a valley that looked to have a small stream running through it. Placing her book beside her, she started to navigate the small decline, wanting to explore more of this marvelous estate.

She couldn't imagine growing up in such surrounds. The village of Sandbach had been small, quaint, but not a lot happened. As for the small cottage her aunt had owned, it had been three bedrooms, a kitchen and drawing room. All modest and little, but comfortable. Her aunt had been a proud woman and had tried her hardest to give them a little luxury while they grew up.

When she'd moved into her sister's London home with the marquess she'd not really understood the divide between the rich and poor. But she did now. The divide was monumental and at times, when they drove through the streets of London, looking out on the poor begging for food or work, she wondered if it would ever be breached.

When she returned to Town she would join a charity and try to give help to those she could. She had been fortunate, had been able to step out of a life of servitude, which she was destined for, into a life of a woman who could choose her future, a husband. So many were not so fortunate.

The walk through the trees down to the small river was cooler than up on the lawn and she pulled her shawl closer about her shoulders. The dappled sunlight lit her way and a crack of a stick made her pause, only to see a deer a few feet away looking at her as if surprised she'd impinged on his solitude.

Sophie continued on working her way through the ferns and undergrowth that had been allowed to grow wild this far away from the house.

The tinkling sound of flowing water met her ears and she pushed through the thick foliage and came to the side of the river. She stifled a gasp and stepped back behind a fern, hoping that Brice had not seen her, for she had certainly seen him, all of him in his naked glory.

Heat infused her face and she lifted her hand, patting her cheek in the hopes of bringing its temperature down. Unable to resist, she peered through the bushes again, watching as he dipped into the water, before coming up again, the water slithering over every ounce of muscle that his body sported.

And there was a lot of muscle, all of it flexing and tightening with each of his movements as he wrung out his hair.

"Do ye like what ye see, lass?"

Sophie gasped, slapping a hand over her mouth. She glanced up at the heavens, wishing right at that moment that she was anywhere but here. She'd been caught ogling him like a little strumpet instead of turning about and heading back toward the house, which is what she should have done the moment she'd intruded on his privacy.

Oh dear Lord in heaven, how would she ever face him again?

She turned around, giving him her back, although she was sure he could not see her well enough to know she'd granted him that modicum of privacy. "I do apologize. I did not know you were here. I should have made my presence known."

She cringed again at being caught. What did he think of her?

"Dinna fret, lass. I dinna mind ye looking. Ye may look as much as ye like."

Sophie bit her lip, counting to five in the hopes that she would not turn around and take her fill some more. He was too tempting for his own good and he damn well knew it.

"Somehow I do not believe that would be appropriate, my lord."

His replying chuckle made her shiver and she shut her eyes, reveling in it a moment. "And our little trysts over the last few days have been appropriate? No one is here and we're hidden from view from the house. What does it matter if ye look at me while we talk?"

Sophie took a calming breath and called his bluff. She turned, stepping through the undergrowth and leaned against a nearby tree watching him. "Happy? I'm looking at you now, my lord."

"Brice, please," he said, walking toward her in the water. The action drew her attention down to his abdomen and the sharp V that delved into the water. She'd never seen a man so naked before and her mind swirled with the idea that he was as naked beneath the water as he was above it.

"Do not come any closer, Brice. Our kissing behind closed doors is one thing, but if you step out of that water and I find you're as naked as I fear you are, that is quite another scenario altogether."

He threw her a mischievous grin and she shook her head. He was impossible! His hands ran along the water's surface and she was envious of them, wanting them upon her body instead.

"Aye, I'm as naked as a babe." He winked and she let out an exasperated sigh. "If you dinna want me to join ye there, why do ye not join me in here? The day is warm, and I'm sure ye have a shift on. That will do. 'Tis what my sister swims in when she partakes in the activity."

Could she go for a swim? She glanced behind her and just as Brice said, the house was hidden from view, and therefore eyes. It had been so many years since she'd swam and here was her chance. Not only that, here was her chance to swim with Brice. She could not turn him down.

She turned back to face him, before reaching up and unbuttoning the top of her gown. "Turn about and let me get undressed."

♛

*B*rice swore, a cold shiver running down his spine with the knowledge that he'd baited Sophie into coming into the water with him.

How the bloody hell would he keep his hands off the lass? The mere thought of her wet, practically naked and near him in the water was enough to make him hard as rock.

If he were a gentleman he would have ignored her presence, finished his swim and left, but he could not. He could not stop himself from talking to her, of asking her to join him. He was a veritable cad.

Should his sister or Elspeth catch them swimming together, scantily dressed and alone, his plans to merge the Mackintosh and Brodie clans would be a dream buried with his parents.

The idea that the lass slowly changing behind him, the sound of clothing being laid over small bushes and slippers being kicked off was also a dream he could not ignore.

He wanted her. Not just here and now, but in his bed tonight, and every night she had left in Scotland. The realization ought to shock sense into him, but it did not. It merely threw images of Sophie into his mind, her hair mussed from their lovemaking, her wide blue orbs sleepy with satisfaction.

Brice fisted his hands at his sides. How the hell was he going to keep his hands off her?

Water sloshed behind him, and he did not turn to look until he was sure her body was fully submerged. "Can I look at ye now, lass?"

"Yes, if you want."

Oh yes, he damn well wanted to... He turned, watching as she walked out a little deeper. The linens from her shift bubbled up from behind her and he caught a glimpse of her upper thigh. The blood in his veins turned molten and he refused to leave the spot on which he stood.

I will not touch her. I will not touch her. I will not touch her.

She laughed, ducking under the water and coming up before him. "Are you not going to swim with me? We can race to the other side if you like."

A race. Perfect. Just the thing to keep his mind and hands off the woman who was driving him to distraction.

"On my count, ready, set..." He dived forward, not waiting to say go and heard her protestations before concentrating on swimming to the other side of the river. It was only a small distance and not deep enough that he could not touch. He made the other side with little effort and turned to see her beside him. "How did ye make it so fast?"

He'd not thought she would keep up. He was a strong swimmer and she was a lass after all. More delicate and unused to such strenuous exercise.

"I swam. I will admit that I think you won, but only just. She stood facing him, her face a little flushed from effort. His heart turned in his chest and he reached for her, unable to keep away.

He tried. God damn it he tried to remain aloof, to not get attached, but it was impossible. She was simply lovely and after years of living in such a secluded location, away from society, his life already mapped out, it was nice to have a little change in his home. Not that his sister and Elspeth were dull, but that they had all grown up together, they were all, including himself, set in their ways and living a life where nothing happened.

A tiresome life if he were honest.

He hoisted her up against his chest. A growl ripped from him as she lifted her legs to wrap about his waist. She didn't shy away from his nakedness, and he didn't hide it from her either. She would only have to glance down and she would see how very much he enjoyed having her in his arms.

"Is this my prize, Laird?" she asked, her voice a whispery purr that made him burn.

She didn't move or undulate against him and, blast it, he wanted her to. He wanted her to seduce him so he didn't feel like the veritable cad who stole the innocence away from the English lass. A woman who was not for him.

What do ye want, lass? The words formed in his mind and he stood still and silent waiting for her to say anything else. He would not ask her, he could not. If he should utter those words and she say *him* there would be no turning back. No denying himself.

He held his body rigid, not willing to let her move or remove herself from his hold. His breath came quick, his heart beating loud in his ears as she slowly closed the space between them and kissed him.

"You may not answer my question, Brice, but I know the answer anyway." She kissed him again, hard and deep, and he didn't try to stop her, didn't push her away, set her down in the water and tell her to leave. That they should not do this.

They were going to do this and he was going to damn well enjoy every minute of it.

He kissed her back, devoured her mouth and clasped the nape of her neck, moving her to his will. Her body slid against his, fitted him like a glove and he groaned when her sex, separated from him by the thinnest of material, pushed against his engorged cock.

It would take little effort to rip up her shift, grab his shaft and slide into her hot, willing body. She gasped against his mouth and he took the opportunity to slide his tongue against hers, loving that she in turn followed his lead and did the same back.

"Ye're so beautiful, Sophie," he whispered against her lips. She threw him a small, seductive smile that would make any man fall to his knees and kissed him back.

The sound of women's voices floated through the trees and he stilled, before tearing Sophie off his body and placing her before him in the water, hoping his body would shield her from view.

"What is it?" she whispered, staring up at him with eyes wide with concern and still hazy with desire.

He pushed down his want of her and mouthed, "People."

She ducked a little in the water and he turned his head as

his sister and Elspeth came to stand on the opposite side of the bank.

The shocked gasp from Elspeth reached him and he was glad to see she had turned around. His sister, however, stared at him with annoyance, her arms crossed over her chest.

"If ye had not forgotten today is my day for the river. Ye may finish yer swim and go," she said, raising one brow.

Brice fought to work out what he could do so no one was ruined here today. Not Sophie's future and not his own with Elspeth. Not that they were engaged, but still, she was who was expected to become the next Lady Mackintosh.

"I only just arrived, Elizabeth. I'll come get ye when I return to the house so ye may come down for a swim." He gave them his back again, hoping that Sophie could not be seen. "I'm naked, so 'tis best if ye leave me be."

Elspeth muttered under her breath and started off, or he assumed she walked off since the sound of leaf litter under feet could be heard. His sister, however, did not move. He cursed the stubborn lass. She was a Mackintosh to the bone.

"I dinna want to swim when the day cools, so I suggest ye get yerself out of the river and home within the next half hour. We'll be in the upstairs drawing room when ye want to let us know that ye're finished."

"Right ye are, lass," he said, not willing to argue with her a moment longer. He just needed her to leave so Sophie could return to the house unharmed and still as innocent as she arrived. He glanced down at her and found her eyes fixed on his manhood that was still painfully aroused and bobbing before her in the water.

Heat rushed his face and he covered himself, having never been more ashamed of himself in his life. What was he doing?! How could he treat her with so little respect? He ought to be horsewhipped.

Her hands came out of the water and covered his, pulling

them away. With just one touch he was back to where he started before they were interrupted and he cursed the fact he'd let her do anything to him, let her ogle and touch him to her heart's content if that is what she wished.

He was going to hell, if he were not there already.

CHAPTER 10

*S*ophie reached out and pulled Brice's hands away, wanting to see what it was that had pressed against her sex.

She was not aware of what men's manhood should look like or what size they came in, but something told her Brice was well-endowed and he knew it. That he knew how to make her want him and to forget all the principles she'd been brought up to follow and adhere to was another matter altogether.

His manhood bobbed in the water, just beneath the surface, but she could see it, its hardness and length. Sophie reached out, running a finger over the tip, sliding it down toward the base. His manhood jumped and she glanced up, her stomach fluttering at the heated, intense stare he bestowed upon her.

She watched him and she clasped her hand about his shaft. She stroked his length and he gasped through clenched teeth. "Did I hurt you?" she asked, releasing him.

He reached out and took her hand, placing it back on his body. "Nay. The opposite, lass."

She bit her lip, touching him again, now taking her time in exploring. The male sex was a curious thing. Hard as steel and yet as soft as velvet. The thought of this long, thick shaft going into her made her legs clench both in fear and need. Obviously such a thing was normal and he would fit. It was what was done after all in marriage and there was no reason they would not work just as well.

His hand came over hers and showed her what to do, to tighten her hold and increase her pace. His stomach muscles clenched and she reached out with her other hand and ran her fingers over his chiseled abdomen.

"We need to stop, lass," he said, his eyes holding hers as she continued to touch him.

Never in her life had she wanted anyone with the need that coursed through her blood right at that moment. She wanted him. Wanted him to lay claim to her. To carry her out of this water, lay her on the bed of grass along the river bank and do wicked, naughty things to her.

"Stop, Sophie," he said, in no way reaching for her hand to stop her. She did not want to either. In fact, had they not been interrupted by his sister and Elspeth she would've allowed him to take her in the water.

His hand came over hers and pulled her away and he stepped back. She glanced up at him and read the determined set of his jaw and knew he'd not let her touch him again. Not here at least.

"I canna let you continue what we're doing. 'Tis not right. Ye need to return to the house before I rip yer innocence from ye without a second thought or care."

The voicing of his wish only made the possibility more alluring, but he was right. Elizabeth and Elspeth would be back here soon and she needed to return to the house before they were caught. It would not do anyone any good to be compromised and she did not want her sister or brother traveling to Scotland to call Brice out for his conduct.

She stood, not caring that her shift had turned transparent or that he could see every curve, every asset of her body. "I will see you at dinner." Sophie dove back toward the opposite side of the river and swam toward where she'd left her clothes. Thankfully Elizabeth and Elspeth had not seen them when they had come down for their swim.

She dressed quickly and left, taking one last glance at Brice through the trees before she disappeared. He stood where she left him, hands clenched at his sides and head bowed. Whatever was he thinking? Or better yet, maybe he ought to stop thinking so much and simply feel. If there was one thing that Sophie was certain of after today, he was right for her. The only man who had ever stirred her heart, mind and body.

Sophie made her way through the trees, sticking to their cover for as long as she could before heading back indoors via the servants' entrance and then stairs lest she run into Elizabeth and have to explain her wet underclothing.

Coming to the upstairs hall, she checked to ensure no one was about and headed for her room. Gretel was there to meet her, and she sighed, a displeased frown creasing her brow when she spied her dishabille.

"I apologize for the state of my clothing. I went for a swim."

Gretel helped her undress, *tsk tsking* as she peeled the layers of clothing off her.

"It's a warm day. Miss Elizabeth came by to see if you wanted to swim with them, but they've only just left so I can only assume you swam alone. That's not safe, Miss Sophie."

Sophie glanced down at her slippers, now ruined from their trek to the river and back. "The river wasn't deep. It was perfectly safe," she lied, not wanting Gretel to know or imagine what happened while she was there. The delectable touches, the kiss that swept her off her feet, the man who'd captured her attention, body and soul.

"I should imagine you're looking forward to returning home after our travels. With the carriage now repaired, we're free to leave for Moy whenever you're ready."

Sophie nodded, lifting her arms as Gretel pulled her shift up over her head. "I've actually invited Jean to come here for a visit. We're not due back in Town for some weeks yet, and with the incident with the carriage I fear our traveling to Skye may not be possible. There is simply not enough time. But Jean may come here for a week or two and then we shall part ways from here."

Gretel laid her wet clothing over her arm, assessing her in the same way Louise did when she was trying to figure out a puzzle. Namely her.

"You've grown attached to the laird," Gretel said, sighing. "I knew you would. The moment you both saw each other I knew there would be trouble."

Sophie frowned, reaching over to her bed and picking up her dressing gown. "And so what if I have grown attached to him. He's eligible, and so am I. There is nothing wrong with that."

"No, there isn't, but do not forget he lives in the middle of nowhere. You swore when you left Sandbach that you would never move to another little hamlet with fewer than one hundred people living in it. I don't mean to speak out of turn, but there are only two people living here plus a handful of servants. I fear if you marry the laird you'll be bored within a week. Not to mention you've only just got back your sister. Have you forgotten you promised her to marry and live close to her in England so you'll never be apart again?"

Sophie slumped onto the bed, having not forgotten, but merely ignoring her own promises. It was true, the laird did live high up in Scotland. Mackintosh land was closer to Inverness than it was to London.

Of course she'd wanted to marry and be close to her sister, but surely Louise would understand that if she loved her husband, she would be happy for her, wherever she was in the world.

"You make me sound fickle. Scotland is beautiful and I should love to live here if that is what my future holds. But a stolen kiss does not equal marriage. You're getting ahead of yourself and above your station."

Gretel raised her brow. "Oh no, you're not going to pull that high-and-mighty stance with me, Sophie Grant. We were equal once and do not forget that I hold the position your sister did before she married the marquess. You've been my oldest friend before nobility got in the way and I'll speak plainly and honestly with you always."

Sophie stood, coming over to Gretel and hugging her. "I'm sorry. I did not mean what I said. I'm just so confused. Brice makes me so muddled that I do not know what I should do."

Gretel pulled her over to the settee and sat beside her. "Please take care, that's all I ask. And do not make any hasty decisions until you've spoken to your family. I like the laird, I do. His sister and their friend also, but heed what I told you some days ago. There is a rumor that he's to wed Miss Elspeth. Promise me that you'll ask him before anything else passes between you. I do not want to see you hurt, that's all."

Sophie clasped Gretel's hands, squeezing them a little. "I will ask him. I promise." A shiver rocked her body and she huddled into the robe. "Please ring for a bath. I'm quite chilled all of a sudden."

Gretel stood, ringing the bell beside the fireplace. "Of course. I'll get your things ready."

Sophie watched her disappear into her dressing room and

she frowned. Gretel was right. She needed to be wary. What did she really know of the laird or his plans for his future? Nothing really. And why was Elspeth here? Of course, they were allied clans, and just like the English they had house parties and stayed at each other's estates, but was her being here because of what Gretel had said before?

Was Elspeth expecting a proposal of marriage?

She shivered at the thought and stood, going to the fire to warm herself. The idea of Brice married to someone else, of taking her in his arms just as he took her today made her stomach twist in knots and left a sour taste in her mouth.

No matter the answer, she needed to find out the truth and then she would know what to do.

Then she would decide if he were worth risking her reputation, gambling her heart and leaving her family behind.

CHAPTER 11

The following evening Sophie sat in the great hall after dinner, warming herself before the fire after a cold change had blown in through the day.

The house, no matter its mammoth size was warm and welcoming and she watched the flames as they licked the wood and turned it slowly to ash.

She'd not seen Brice all day and he'd been absent from dinner the night before. Sophie wasn't certain what to make of it. Was he avoiding her, or after Gretel's words yesterday, was she reading into situations and circumstances more than she ought?

Elspeth too was still in residence and twice today it had been on Sophie's tongue to try to gauge why she was a guest here. Was there an understanding between the families?

A shadow passed over her and she glanced up to see Brice standing before her, his trews damp, his boots mud-splattered.

She glanced at him, not moving, and he stared back and all thoughts of leaving him alone, of not touching him again, flew right out of her mind. He closed the space between them, wrenched her out of her seat and kissed her.

Hard.

Sophie melted against him, wrapping her arms about his waist. She kissed him back with as much passion as she could summon. Heedless of where they were or who could walk in on them at any moment, the kiss went on, her body aching for things no well-bred young lady ought to want.

He clasped her chin and tilted her head to kiss her deep. She moaned when he stepped into her, pushing his hardness against her stomach.

"I missed ye today," he said, breaking the kiss.

She took a calming breath, nodding. "I missed you too."

He shook his head, scowling. "I canna stay away from ye. I've tried. I canna do it."

Sophie licked her lips, unable to hide the pleasure his words brought forth. Her body felt as though it were on fire, alive and burning for the man before her.

"I want you too," she said, having never uttered anything so scandalous or truthful to a man before in her life. Brice was a laird, a gentleman, he would not hide anything from her. Gretel was wrong. The rumors were wrong.

"When can we be alone?" she asked, wanting him to say now. Follow me and we'll be alone right now.

He glanced behind himself and stepped back. "I will not ruin ye, Sophie. No matter how tempting ye are or how much I want ye in my bed."

She shivered at the thought. Now that she'd seen him naked, to picture him above her on a soft bed, his strong, muscled body pinning her down made her body ache. "And if I want you to? What then?"

He sighed, running a hand through his hair. A muscle worked in his jaw before he said, "Dinna tempt me, lass. I'm drawing every ounce of honor I have not to take ye whenever I see ye about the house. Ye're literally driving me mad."

She grinned, the fact that she drove him to distraction was a welcome reprieve for he drove her mad as well. "It's my choice, is it not? What if I choose you?"

He reached out, running a hand across her cheek, one finger trailing across her lips before he let it fall to his side. "Ye cannot."

Sophie raised her brow. "We'll see about that."

"See about what?" Elspeth asked, coming into the room, a book held against her chest.

Sophie didn't move, but she could not say the same about Brice. He started at the sound of Elspeth's voice and couldn't look more guilty if he tried. She smiled at Elspeth before taking her seat again. "We thought we may take a ride tomorrow, if the weather turns back to being pleasant. I was merely saying we'll have to see about it."

Elspeth nodded, glancing out the window before seating herself beside Sophie and opening her book. "I'll not be riding. Have ye forgotten that Mama will be arriving tomorrow, Brice? She'll want to see ye, of course."

Brice's face paled before he smiled. "Nay, of course I had not forgotten. We can ride after yer mother arrives if ye do wish to come. She normally travels in the morning in any case."

"Hmm, yes, she does," Elspeth said, her tone disinterested and bored. "But no, I shall stay here. Thank ye for the invitation though."

Brice bowed, inching back toward the door. "I'll see ye at dinner," he said to them both. Sophie leaned back in the settee, wondering why he was a little unsettled by the news of Elspeth's mother's arrival. Maybe there was an understanding between them. But how could she ask such a question without looking like a woman who was seeking her own proposal?

It was such a private thing to query about that she would have to figure out another way to ask in a roundabout way. Elspeth chuckled at something in her book and Sophie glanced at the young woman. She was pretty in her own way, her red hair long and curly, bringing out the green in her eyes. But there was something about her that didn't fit with Brice. They were friends, that she had no doubt, but there was no spark, no desire. Not like when she was around him.

Just the thought of having him near her made her shiver and ache with need. His voice gave her lascivious ideas, and as for his wicked mouth and hands, well, she would never tire of those on her body.

None of that would matter if he was going to marry someone else. As for that institution, Sophie wasn't certain she wanted to live so very far away from her family should he ask. There were many obstacles to work through should they align their families. If only he lived in London, then he would never be rid of her and the choice to marry him would be as easy as breathing.

*B*rice stood out in front of his home, Elspeth at his side, her arm linked with his as her mother's carriage rolled down the drive and before the castle doors.

Elspeth had taken after her father in looks and mannerisms and was the opposite to what her mother was like. In the woman's youth she'd been a reputed beauty that even his own father had courted before his beloved mama had won his heart.

A footman opened the carriage door and Brice helped her

down and kissed her cheek. "Welcome, Lady Brodie. 'Tis good to have ye here with us again."

She slapped his chest playfully, turning to her daughter. "Enough with the Lady Brodie, Brice. Ye know my name is Margaret."

He smiled as she kissed her daughter, before they headed indoors, chatting to themselves. He followed behind into the great hall where they had set up a small repast for lunch before they headed out on their afternoon ride.

Sophie and Elizabeth were already in the hall and he couldn't help the small twitch of his lips at seeing her again. Every time he saw her something in his chest tightened and he was starting to think for the very first time in his life he'd fallen for a lass.

And not just any lass, but an English one at that. She watched him, her wide, blue eyes glistening with amusement and knowledge that only they shared. A mutual understanding of enjoyment, of attraction.

For he certainly felt that for the lass. To the point where he'd tell his family and Elspeth's to go to Hades so he could have the one woman who made him burn.

"This is Miss Sophie Grant, Mama. She's the Marquess Graham's sister-in-law. She's staying here from London."

Sophie curtsied and smiled at Margaret. Lady Brodie's demeanor changed within an instant, cooled and became more aloof than he'd ever seen before.

"Miss Grant. How fortuitous that you are here. I understand from my daughter's letters that you'll be leaving us soon, heading farther into the highlands, I understand."

"Ah, not any more, my lady. I fell over on my first day here in the village and injured myself. The laird and Miss Elizabeth were kind enough to allow me to stay here while I recovered, but the delay has stopped me from being able to visit my friend in Skye. I do hope however that she can travel here for a stay."

Margaret laughed, a tinkling sound that oozed condescension. "The guest is now inviting other guests to stay." She turned to Brice, her smile brittle. "Has the Laird of Mackintosh been taken in, I wonder."

His sister glanced at him wide-eyed and he counted to five before replying lest he set one of his family's oldest friends back in her carriage and send her on her way. "'Twas my idea to invite Miss Grant's friend to stay. We're loath to see her leave and wished to prolong her visit here as much as we could."

Sophie threw him a thankful smile as Elizabeth clasped her hand.

"Shall we have some tea?" he asked, wanting to change the subject.

"I think a whiskey will do me better," Margaret said, her tone cold. She sat on a nearby chair and glanced at them all as if she were the matriarch here. "Miss Grant, yer sister married very well. When I heard of yer particulars I wrote to my friend in London. She informed me yer elder sister was a lady's companion and now here ye are, a guest at an earl's home. Ye must be well-pleased."

"Mama," Elspeth said. Her mother gave Elspeth a quelling glance and she sat, her lips thinning in concern.

"I'm very pleased for her, my lady. She married the man she loved, which can never be a fault."

Margaret raised her brow. "Ach, but does the marquess love her in return? 'Tis all very well to love one's husband, but these London marriages are never happy ones. Too much diversion, too many temptations. I'm very well-pleased that we live where we do. Ye may keep yer town life, Miss Grant. 'Tis not for a Scot."

"I for one enjoyed London when I traveled there," Elizabeth said, taking Sophie and seating her on a settee a little distance away from Lady Brodie. A fortunate thing since the woman had released her claws and was wanting to scratch Sophie's eyes out from the looks of it.

"I agree, Elizabeth. I think London would do me very well should I travel there." He winked at Sophie and she smiled at him. Once again it was as if the sun came out and warmed his soul. There was no use for it, he was besotted with her and now he had to figure out what the hell he was going to do about it.

"You are both more than welcome at the marquess's home in London or Ashby House, which is in Kent, should you ever visit us."

"And here ye are yet again, Miss Grant. Inviting people to homes that are not yer own."

"Lady Brodie, that is unkind. Ye will apologize to Miss Grant," he said, his tone brooking no argument.

Her ladyship's mouth puckered up as if she'd eaten something sour. Brice held her gaze, not willing to have Sophie insulted through no fault of her own. She could not help who her sister married, and he was sure from the way Sophie spoke of her siblings that they were very close, and any friend of Sophie's was a friend of theirs.

He frowned. Had Lady Brodie sensed his and Sophie's connection? She'd certainly fixated on Sophie from the moment she arrived. Had Elspeth written to her ladyship of her concerns? The horror on Elspeth's face right now after her mother's atrocious behavior would make one think not.

"I apologize, Miss Grant. Ye must make allowances for my blunt tongue. 'Tis a Scottish habit I never grew out of." Lady Margaret stood. "Come, Brice, there are things to discuss."

She started for the door and Brice bowed before following the harridan out into the corridor. Something told him the things to discuss were exactly the things he wanted to avoid.

CHAPTER 12

"What is the meaning of this lass being here and the looks that ye both keep throwing each other? I'll not have it, Brice. Ye're to wed Elspeth and ye know it. 'Tis what ye agreed to before yer parents died."

Brice sat behind his desk, hating that what she said was all true and cursing himself for the bloody fool he was in having promised such a thing when under stress from his parents' illnesses.

"Ye know that I care for Elspeth and should she agree, of course I'll marry her, but the marriage will not be one of affection. Not in the way that a marriage should be. Is that what ye want for yer daughter? Dinna ye want her to marry the man she loves, not merely respects?" Certainly after being with Sophie, he couldn't think of anything worse than marrying a woman he did not desire every minute of every day and respect her opinion. Sophie was both delectable and intelligent, enjoyable to be around. She was certainly no simpering miss who would make his teeth ache from clenching.

"Bollocks. Elspeth cares for ye a great deal and should ye

turn yer head her way ye'd see that. Ye need to send the English lass home and ye need to do it soon before she starts to get ideas into her head that ye are going to offer her marriage. Dinna think I've forgotten why ye have this grand home still in yer hands. 'Tis because of the Brodies and their blunt."

"And the loan has been paid back in full with interest, need I remind ye." He loathed that his parents had asked for help, and yet at the same time he was grateful still to have Mackintosh Castle in the family.

"Agreements were made as well as money passing between hands that day. Dinna forget yer promise, Brice. Yer parents would roll over in their graves should they know ye were playing with a Sassenach."

He rubbed a hand over his jaw, the thought of Sophie going back to London haunted him. For her to be courted and admired, married to someone else made the blood in his veins chill. He glanced out the window, anywhere but at lady Brodie and her all-seeing eyes and viperish mouth.

"Her carriage is repaired and she is healed from her injury. I'm certain that Miss Grant will not be with us for too much longer." Bile rose in his throat at his words. How would he ever send her away? To watch her carriage roll down the drive, out of his life forever made him want to punch something. Hard.

"Good, for I would hate to see a young Scottish lord such as yerself throw away yer future happiness on a Sassenach. Marriage to my daughter, as both her and yer parents wished is best for this area and our clans. We must keep the Scottish bloods in the highlands pure. 'Tis a good match with Elspeth," she said, her tone cajoling. "Ye'll see. In time ye'll learn to love her."

Brice didn't want to learn to do anything, certainly not

how to love someone. What a cold, unfeeling marriage he would have if that were the case.

Damn his idiot younger self for promising such a thing to his parents. It would be a mistake he would live with for the rest of his life.

Lady Brodie stood, starting toward the door like a warrior facing battle.

"Lady Brodie," he called out, halting her steps. She turned, facing him. "Dinna be rude to Miss Grant again. Ye may hail from Clan Brodie, which has been our closest ally for hundreds of years, but I'll not have any guest under my roof shamed simply because she's walked into a situation not of her making." He gave her ladyship a pointed stare. "Do ye understand?"

She gave one sharp nod. "Understood, so long as ye understand as well."

"I do," he said, watching the door close behind her ladyship and close on any hope he harbored that his future could be different than what had been planned.

꧁꧂

Sophie secluded herself up on the tower roof with the book on Scottish clans and looked at who Clan Mackintosh had married over the years. All she could find were other clan names, and information. It seemed Clan Mackintosh only married Scots and never the English, never a Sassenach from over the border.

She placed it down on the small blanket she sat upon and glanced out over the lands. Lady Brodie hated her. It was an undisputed fact and no matter how much Elizabeth and Elspeth tried to dismiss her notion, Sophie knew it to be true.

But why?

That was the question she was asking herself. Why would anyone take an instant dislike of someone unless they were threatened by them? She brought her knees up against her chest and leaned on them. Maybe what Gretel had been saying was true. The two families were meant to join through the marriage of Brice and Elspeth.

Not that that made any sense, for Elspeth showed very little interest in Brice, she showed Sophie more notice than him. Brice certainly liked the woman, but there was no chemistry between the two. Not that she'd ever seen.

She sighed. She would have to talk to Brice and listen to what he said. She should not have been kissing him if he were betrothed to another. Not that she thought that he was. He would not act so shamelessly.

"I've been looking all over the house for ye, lass. Are ye all right? I'm sorry about Lady Brodie. She can be hard toward strangers and, well, English ones more than most."

Sophie glanced at him, not moving from her position. "She doesn't like me, which is fine."

Ask him Sophie. Ask him now.

But how could she ask him something so personal? She shut her eyes, willing herself to be strong.

Brice came and sat beside her, leaning back against the stone wall. "The last week that ye have been here has been one of the best weeks of my life. I'll miss ye when ye go."

Go? So he expected her to leave still. She could not ask him now what was between him and Elspeth. How could she when he certainly saw no future with her?

Pain tore through her chest at the thought of leaving him. Of returning home and not seeing his wickedly handsome and teasing face across the table each morning where he'd wink and grin and make her smile.

"I will miss you too." She would not lie. She would miss him. Terribly so. "I think it's best that I leave as soon as the letter from Jean arrives. I have doubts that she'll come, but I hope you won't mind if she does."

He shook his head, reaching out to take her hand. His warm, gloveless fingers ran over her flesh and shot goose-bumps across her skin. "Nay, ye are both welcome, for as long as ye like."

If only that were true... Sophie sat back and stared at nothing in particular, her mind a whirr of thoughts of wants and means.

He clasped her jaw and turned her to face him. She lost herself in the dark-green depths of his eyes full of longing that she too could acknowledge. Not willing to leave without experiencing what it would be like to have someone whom you loved, Sophie closed the space between them and kissed him.

It was a gamble, a risk, but she could not leave without having this just once more.

He met her halfway, taking her lips in a kiss that made her toes curl in her silk slippers. She reached up, clasping his shoulders and kissed him back with as much passion as he. His lips moved across hers, took and played with her mouth until she did not know what to do or what she wanted.

Well, she knew what she wanted. She wanted Brice.

He broke the kiss, standing and pulling her up with him. He didn't say a word and she did not ask him, for deep down she knew where he was going. They climbed back down the tower stairs, entered the passage that ran along his side of the house and walked toward his chambers.

Nerves fluttered in her stomach and she clasped her abdomen, unsure suddenly if she were ready for this. He stopped at the door and turned to face her. Sophie read the question in his eyes and determination straightened her spine. She reached past him and opened the door, swinging it wide before pushing against his chest and walking him backward into the room.

She shut the door and turned the lock. Tamping down her nervousness, she twisted around and gave him her back. "Can you help me with my ties?"

A light brush of his lips against her shoulder and she reached behind, clasping his face. "Clothes first, my lord, then you may kiss me again."

He chuckled, a low gravelly sound and she knew she'd never tire of him. Never not want him.

His nimble fingers made short work of her ties, pushing her gown to pool at her feet before her shift, stockings and slippers all followed soon after. Her body shook as she turned to face him, naked as the day she was born and so ready to be with the man before her.

The man she loved.

Sophie reached up and slipped his cravat loose, throwing it to the floor with her gown. She allowed her hands to drop over his chest and abdomen, taking pains to enjoy every facet of his body. His breathing was ragged as she pulled his shirt out of his breeches, sliding it up over his head to visually enjoy him as much as she physically could.

She devoured him, taking in every delectable thing about his chest, the small smattering of hair, his flat stomach and bulging pants.

Sophie bit her lip when she looked at the size of his manhood. He seemed even larger than he did in the lake and trepidation skittered down her spine that they may not fit.

"Damn it all to hell." He swooped her up in his arms, closing the gap to the bed in only a few strides. She let out a little squeak when he threw her on the bed and she bounced once before he came down over her, pushing her into the thick, warm bedding.

"The way ye look at me. 'Tis too much." He kissed her,

stopping her from replying. Sophie took the opportunity to show him instead of saying just how much he affected her as well. How he was too much and not enough. That she would never have enough of him.

Their lips took a life of their own, both seeking, taking and teasing the other. Somewhere in the back of her mind a warning voice urged caution, but she could not. If she were to leave, then she would have this once. Lay with the man she loved. It would sustain her for the rest of her days and whatever future she had before her.

Her fingers skimmed down his smooth back, running over his bottom before reaching between them and undoing the buttons on the front. He moaned, urging her to touch him. He needn't. She wanted to touch the hard yet velvety skin of his manhood.

She clasped him firmly and rolled her thumb across the top of his phallus. He pushed into her hold and she grinned. To have him at her mercy was a heady thing.

He threw her a wicked grin and kissed her before setting little bites down her neck, her chest, paying homage to each of her nipples. His tongue slid against the puckered flesh and little electrical shots pulsated to her core. Sophie writhed beneath him, pushing her body into him, silently begging for him to take her.

"Soon, love," he whispered against her stomach, kissing her lower still until the warmth of his breath fluttered across her mons. She stilled at the ministration.

"What are you doing?" she hissed, trying to sit up a little.

He pushed her back down, pinching one of her nipples and making her gasp. "Tasting ye."

Sophie wasn't sure what he meant, but when his tongue slid across her flesh in the most private of her places, his words became perfectly clear and not for anything would she stop him. For his clever mouth was once again driving her to distraction.

$\mathcal{B}$rice didn't know how he had allowed a kiss to lead them here, but now that he had Sophie in his bed, he'd never let her go. Not for family duty or expectation, not even for his clansmen. Somewhere along the way, he'd fallen in love with the lass and there was no going back now.

He tasted her with his tongue, teased her flesh until she was writhing in his hands, her fingers spiking through his hair and holding him right where she liked.

He liked it too. He teased her, pulled her close to her release and then took it away, inwardly enjoying himself immensely and wanting to prolong their time together. He didn't want to go back to the real world. He wanted to stay here forever. In Sophie's arms and in bed.

"Please, Brice." His name was but a gasp and he came back up over her, using his hand to tease her sensitive flesh. "Do ye like me touching ye here, lass?"

He slid one finger into her wet heat and she gasped, closing her legs about his arms.

"Yes," she breathed. "Please, I want you."

The words were precisely what he wanted to hear. He moved his hips to between her legs, guiding himself into her. She opened for him like a flower before the sun. He moaned as he slid into her, breaking her maidenhead, careful not to hurt her too much.

"I dinna want to hurt ye, lass." He paused, giving her time to accommodate him.

She stared up at him, her eyes clouded with lust. "It's not too bad. Please do not stop."

Brice took his time before he sheathed himself fully. She was warm, and so damn tight. His balls ached for release.

"Ye are so beautiful, lass."

She reached up, pulling him down and taking his lips. He thrust into her and she moaned against his mouth, making his cock rock hard. He tupped her fast, pinning her down. The need to see her come apart in his arms, to shatter before him was his whole focus.

Her legs came up about his hips, one sliding over his back and he clasped her thigh, pushing deeper still, harder. She allowed him take his fill as he brought her ever closer to release.

She thrashed under him, helping him to ride her and he'd fought not to lose himself. Her fingers scratched down his back, her core tightening even more about his cock.

"Come for me. Fuck, lass, come," he demanded, his need overwhelming him.

She gasped his name and he kissed her, masking her sounds as she contracted about his cock, spiking his own orgasm and milking him for all he had.

He slumped beside her after a time, both their breathing ragged. Brice rubbed a hand over his brow, feeling the light sheen of sweat there. "Are ye alright, lass? I wasn't too rough?"

She rolled over, coming to lie in the crook of his arm. He glanced down at her and his heart thumped loud in his chest. She was all softness, sweetness that he never wanted to part from. "No. You were perfect."

No. *She* was perfect and he was a perfect bastard for taking her innocence. But what was the problem with that when she would be his wife? He would not let her go. Not now. No matter what Clan Brodie thought on the matter.

CHAPTER 13

*T*he following morning Sophie floated about her room, her mind whirring with thoughts about Brice, of what he'd done to her yesterday afternoon and how they'd secluded themselves away, oblivious if they were missed or caught.

Her sister would skin her alive should she know what she'd done, but what was a little scandal when one was in love? And if anything was proven to her yesterday it was that she was in love with Laird Mackintosh.

She took a calming breath as her stomach fluttered with the acknowledgment of such a fact. Soon she would join the family for breakfast and see him again. After their actions she could not see any other possibility for them but to be married. Not that she'd lain with him to force his hand, but surely one could not say such sweet things, touch with such reverence and not care. Not want that person in their life always.

Sophie dabbed a little bit of rosemary on her neck and stood, taking one last look at herself in the mirror. "I will see you before luncheon, Gretel," she said, watching as Gretel came out of the dressing room with two of her gowns in her hands.

"Have a good morning," her friend said, sitting before the fire with what looked like needle and thread.

"I will." Sophie started down the long hallway, excitement thrumming through her. She didn't come across anyone on her way to the dining room, but upon entering it she knew something was wrong.

Elizabeth sat staring at her brother, her face ashen and Elspeth did not look much better. As for Lady Brodie she was blotchy and red. Sophie's steps halted. Was her ladyship angry or upset? When she turned, she knew what she was.

She was furious.

"Good morning," she said, continuing into the room and hoping she'd misread the situation.

"Is it true, Sophie?" Elspeth asked, tears brimming in her eyes.

Sophie looked to Elizabeth and then Brice for clarification. Brice looked to Elspeth, sighing. "I've already told ye the truth. No need to ask Sophie about it."

"Miss Grant, need I remind ye, young man," Lady Brodie said, her voice cold and hard.

Sophie folded her hands in her lap, unsure if everyone had found out what they were up to yesterday, or if Brice had declared something that she wasn't aware of.

"Was this yer plan all the time?" Elspeth asked, her eyes now as hard as her mother's. "To come here and land yerself a rich husband? Were there not enough Englishmen in England falling at yer feet that ye had to throw yerself at my betrothed?"

Sophie gasped, looking to Brice. "You are engaged?" The room spun and she clasped the chair, hoping she'd not topple off.

"I'm not engaged, Sophie," he said, turning back to Lady Brodie. "I never proposed to Elspeth."

"Posh," her ladyship snapped back. "It was expected. Wanted by both clans and ye dare come here this morning and tell me after our discussion yesterday that ye've changed yer mind. I'll not have it, and nor will I let ye make a mockery of our family name or our child."

Sophie looked to Elizabeth and the sadness she read in her friend's eyes gave her pause. The union between Brice and Elspeth was expected all this time, and he'd dallied with her and she'd let him.

She cringed, shame washing through her. "I did not know," she said, her eyes burning all of a sudden.

"Sophie, 'tis an old desire of my parents and Elspeth's too that was made when they were ill."

"Dinna ye be forgetting that Clan Brodie saved this stronghold financially so ye may inherit. What a way to thank yer friends. Throw a beautiful, strong Scottish woman out with the pig scraps for an English whore."

"Do not insult Miss Grant again, Lady Brodie or I'll be kicking yer ass out with the pig scraps as well," he roared.

Sophie jumped in her chair, unable to comprehend what had happened. The day had started off so beautifully and now? Now it was what nightmares were made of.

"May I see you in your office, my lord?" she asked, standing and glad that her legs didn't buckle under her. She fled the room, further insults flying at her back from Lady Brodie and the sound of Elizabeth's voice consoling her ladyship and Elspeth.

Sophie made the laird's office and went and stood beside the roaring fire, her body shivered and felt chilled to the bone.

Brice followed her, shutting the door as he strode in. "Sophie, I'm sorry. I dinna think they'd take my declaration to marry ye this morning so hard. Ye didn't deserve such treatment."

Sophie shook her head, not able to comprehend how he thought any of this was tolerable. "Did you allow the Brodie clan to think that you would offer for their daughter and only changed your mind when I came here?"

He glanced down at the floor, his inability to meet her gaze telling. "'Tis difficult to understand. There may have been a hope between the families, but I never offered marriage to Elspeth. I want to marry ye, Sophie," he said, finally looking at her. "I want ye."

"You only want me because your mind is still addled from yesterday. Had I not fallen over in Moy and hurt myself, and then been offered hospitality here, would you have married Elspeth?"

He ran a hand over his jaw, taking his time in answering her. "There is a possibility that would have occurred, aye."

Sophie shook her head, ice running through her veins. What a fool she'd been. She'd risked so much, had trusted him and this is what was happening all the time. "You bastard. How could you? How could you chase me, allow me to think there may be a future between us when all the time you were planning on offering to Elspeth?"

He reached for her and she slapped his hands away. "When? When did you decide that it was me that you wanted, and don't you dare lie to me, Brice."

A muscle ticked in his jaw before he said, "Yesterday."

Bile rose in Sophie's throat and she clasped her stomach, scared she was going to cast up her accounts all over his highly polished wood floor. He came to her, taking her hand and she pushed him away, stumbling toward the door.

"You decided you wanted me," she said rounding on him. "After you'd had your way with me. What was I to you, some plaything? A little English diversion before you settled down with your Scottish lass? Or did I merely meet with your exalted bedding standard and Elspeth did not? If you tell me that you had similar relations with her I fear my actions will not be my own."

He held out a hand, placating her. "Nay, never, Sophie. I would not do that. Please understand, I did not think I'd meet anyone like ye. I canna think of anyone I want to spend the rest of my life with more than ye."

Sophie stared at him, and damn it, a small part of her wanted to believe what he said. That duty was his only path forward until she had arrived and he'd fallen for her. But never had he talked of the future, only that he would miss her when she left. Surely had he planned for them to be together he would have spoken of dreams, of a future with them here in Scotland. But he had not. He'd not mentioned the word love at all.

She was a fool.

"I do not believe you. You're not who I thought you were. I'm going back to my room to pack. I'll be leaving today."

"Sophie, no, please." He strode over to her, taking her hands. "Please believe me. I dinna mean to hurt you or Elspeth." He shook his head, seemingly struggling to find the right words. "I did not know that I would meet a lass that would make me question my word, my promise to my parents."

She pulled out of his grasp and started for the door. "But you did hurt me, didn't you, and your promise to your parents was broken the moment you first kissed me, so I do not want to hear such excuses." Sophie shut the door behind her, her legs felt heavy and unstable, and using the staircase bannister she slowly made her way back to her room.

The house about her blurred with unshed tears and she bit the inside of her cheek to stop herself from crying before the few servants she passed.

However would she face Louise? However would she face her future husband, whomever he may be now that she was ruined? No one would have her now. A little chiding voice beat against her ear, telling her what a fool she was, a silly country miss who had stepped into a world she wasn't prepared for and had lost.

And the voice was right and so too Gretel. Too blinded by her feelings for the laird, she could not see or hear what was happening right before her. That he had played them both and she'd lost the game.

Damn Scots. She would never trust another.

CHAPTER 14

*S*pring ended and so too did summer in the highlands and the first snows of the season had started to fall and stick. It would be a cold winter this year, a hard winter. Not that he expected anything else. He deserved to be isolated, cold and lonely, especially after what had occurred in the spring when Sophie had been a guest here.

The thought of her, as usual, sent pain to coil in the vicinity of his heart. He leaned back in his chair, shutting his eyes, wanting to picture her as they were the day before she'd left. Warm in his arms, gazing at him with such adoration and trust that he'd never want for another.

He shook his head. He'd made a right mess of things and true to her word she'd packed up the day after he'd taken her to his bed and hightailed it back to London. Her friend had written stating she could not come, which was fortunate as Sophie had left in any case, and he would not have known what to say to the woman had she arrived.

A light knock sounded at his door and his sister peeped around the threshold. "May I come in?"

He gestured for her to enter, sitting up to lean over his

desk. "Of course. What is it ye wanted to talk to me about, Elizabeth?"

She held a missive in her hand. Her demeanor, the worry lines about her eyes made him pause. "What is it, lass? Has there been bad news?"

Elizbeth worked her bottom lip and he was about to expire before she said, "I dinna want to tell ye before, but I've been corresponding with Sophie the whole time she has been back in England. I've had news today from her."

Everything in his body came to life at the sound of her name aloud. Elizabeth had not mentioned Sophie to him, not since the day she had left. "What does she write?"

Does she ask of me? Is she well? Is she happy?

"She's betrothed to be married."

"The hell she is." He surged to his feet, sending his chair backward to crack on the mahogany floor. "To whom?"

"Does it matter?" Elizabeth said, watching him warily. "Ye let her go."

He gaped at his sibling, having never heard her say something to him like that before, cutting and condescending as if Sophie's leaving was his fault.

Well, aye, it was his fault, but he had tried to get her to stay. To believe what he was saying. He'd been a fool, a blind idiot, but he would have married her. Would have loved her had she only given him a chance.

"Ye let her believe that ye never loved her. Did ye tell her before she left or did ye allow her to return to England thinking ye'd ruined her without a shadow of shame upon yer soul?"

Brice stilled at Elizabeth's words. "Ye knew?" He strode to the window, ripping the curtains back to see outside.

"Of course I knew ye'd ruined her. She all but glowed the morning she walked into the breakfast room and before Lady Brodie tanned yer hide, ye too looked like a cat who'd licked the cream." Elizabeth shook her head at him, her eyes hard with annoyance. "Ye need to fix this problem before it's too late."

He nodded absently, his mind running through everything that he needed to accomplish to get to London by the fastest means possible. "I never told her. She was so angry that I did not think it would make a difference. I was wrong." He turned to face his sister. "I won't let Sophie marry anyone else, not unless that anyone is me."

Elizabeth stood and joined him at the windows. She smiled, another thing he'd not seen for some months. His sister had been angry at him and consequently given him the silent treatment ever since Sophie and Elspeth had departed.

He'd thought Elizabeth had blamed him for Elspeth running away to the continent to travel abroad, but he couldn't help but wonder if Elspeth had been more than pleased by the turn of events. Not initially, but certainly when her lady's maid had mentioned such a trip abroad, she'd been only too willing to travel with her.

Lady Brodie however had promised retribution, but really there was little she could do other than become a rival clan. Clan Mackintosh no longer owed anyone anything, and no one would be calling in a favor on him in the forthcoming future.

He was free to travel to London and get his lass back. And that was exactly what he was going to do. "Wish me luck," he said, kissing Elizabeth on the cheek and heading for the door.

"Good luck, brother."

He ignored her parting comment that he would need it.

CHAPTER 15

London

Sophie wrung her hands before her as she paced in her bedroom. Today she would marry Mr. Mathew Fitzgerald, a childhood friend from Sandbach who was training to be a barrister, and a man who did not evoke one ounce of desire in her, no matter how much he tried with his kisses.

He had come up to Town, wanting to visit Stephen whom he'd not seen for some years and they had been thrown together. Heartsick and missing Brice, Sophie had perhaps shown more notice than she really felt toward the gentleman, and within a month he'd proposed and shockingly she'd said yes.

"Why did I do such a thing?" she said aloud in her room to no one. She was alone, wanting to have the few hours before she gave herself to a man who was suffocating in his attention toward her, that had only become worse after she'd agreed to be his wife. "This is a disaster."

Her vision blurred and she swiped up her handkerchief from her dressing table, dabbing at her cheeks. Damn Brice and damn Clan Brodie and everyone who thought that the laird of Mackintosh would make a great match to a woman whose only asset was that she was Scottish.

They certainly did not love each other, but then he'd never told her that he loved her either so her point was moot.

She missed him.

Sophie slumped on the bed, fighting the need to curl into a ball and never go anywhere ever again. She'd written to Elizabeth, part in hope that she would give news of her impending nuptials to Brice. But today was her wedding day, and she'd not heard back from Elizabeth or seen her fiery-red Scot since the day she left.

He did not care.

She supposed Brice would be married now to Elspeth. She ought to thank Elizabeth for not telling her such news for to read it in black and white that Brice would never be hers would've been a heartbreak she could not have faced.

But she did have to face it. He was gone and she was about to marry a man who loved her, or at least, liked her very much.

A commotion downstairs sounded and she stood, going to the door and opening it. Yelling sounded from the foyer and Sophie stilled when the very distinct and very demanding Scottish burr reached her ears.

Brice!

She shut her mouth with a snap, unsure whether she should go and see what he wanted or hide. What was he doing here? Did he come to wish her well, to apologize and show that marriage to other people was the right course? Was Elspeth with him?

Her fingers clenched the handle, but her feet refused to

move. Not that they had to for Brice appeared at the top of the stairs and, looking about to see which way to go, spied her.

"Sophie," he said, the sound of her name on his lips was like a balm over a festering wound.

"Brice. What are you doing here?" she asked, coming out into the corridor to meet him. He took her hands, glancing behind him. Her brother-in-law came into view at the top of the stairs, yelling out to Brice.

Brice wrenched her back into her room, the snick of the lock putting an end to Luke interrupting them.

"Sophie, let me in and I'll escort Laird Mackintosh outside."

"I'd like to see him try," Brice said, his voice brooking no argument.

Sophie sighed. "It's okay, my lord. I will speak to Laird Mackintosh. I will be down shortly."

There was a small delay before the muffled sound of Luke's voice met her ears. "Very well. I'll be in the library with Louise when you're ready."

She turned back to Brice, unable to stop herself from taking in all his grandeur. He looked travel-weary, his clothes dusty and rumpled. His hair was longer and he'd not bothered to tie it back and so it sat upon his shoulders, the red, fiery locks making her want to run her hands through it, pull him toward her and kiss him.

She'd missed him so much.

Sophie stepped back, needing space to think straight. He had a way of discombobulating her. "Why are you here, Brice? Should you not be in Scotland with your wife?"

He reared back at her words. "I dinna have a wife, lass, not yet at least. Did Elizabeth not tell ye what happened after ye left?"

He wasn't married? Hope and despair ran through her at

the declaration. He wasn't married, but she was to be soon and so it was too late.

Wasn't it?

"Elizabeth never mentioned you at all." Not that she'd wanted to hear of his marriage, of where they had traveled for their honeymoon. Just the thought of Brice lying with another woman made her head ache. For weeks after leaving Scotland she'd had nightmares of such a scene, of him kissing Elspeth and consummating the marriage. Of stealing kisses such as he had with her, but instead of Sophie in the dreams, it had been Elspeth, her mother's mocking voice whispering in her ear that she was nothing but common English nonsense.

"I dinna marry Elspeth. In fact, I asked them to leave the same day ye departed for London." He reached for her and she edged away. If he touched her, she'd be lost and she had Mathew to marry. A good man who was right now getting ready in another part of the marquess's home. Brice and his distraction were not needed.

"I should have come after ye, to tell ye how sorry I am. I'll admit, I should never had dallied with ye, stolen kisses that were not for me, but the day that I found ye on the tower I'd made up my mind to marry ye, lass. I want ye to marry me still." His eyes beseeched her and her heart beat loud in her ears. "I love ye, Sassenach. You're the only lass I want beside me for the rest of my days, however many that will be."

Sophie swiped at her cheek, biting the inside of her lip to distract herself from all the wonderful things he was saying. "You should have told me what your family expected of you. Had you just said that it wasn't what you wanted, all those stolen kisses would not have felt like lies."

"I'm sorry, lass. I was stupid."

"You were, but then you are a man…"

He grinned, that devilishly handsome smile, and she knew the fight was lost. She loved him. Loved him still. Senseless, obstinate Scot that he was. "I never said I was an angel, lass, but one kiss from ye, one look, and there was no way that I was going to let ye go. Tell me ye'll marry me." He stepped before her, and this time she didn't step away when he reached to hold her.

She sighed at being back in his arms. It was like coming home. Perfect and right in every way. "I'm marrying Mr. Fitzgerald today," she stated, wanting him to grovel for just a little longer.

"No ye are not. Ye're going to marry me instead. Say yes."

Sophie raised her brow. "We have a whole wedding planned today. Guests will be arriving soon. Why, Mathew is only a few doors away getting ready." She gestured to herself. "If you haven't noticed I'm in a wedding gown."

He glanced down at the blue silk gown with overlaying lace and his gaze darkened. "Say yes, Sophie, to my question. I'll not be taking no for an answer. Ye know ye love me as much as I love ye. If ye marry whatever his name is ye'll regret it and I'll have to force ye to have a lifelong affair with me. Now, ye dinna want to do that, do ye?"

No she did not want to do that, and although she would hurt Mathew she knew that to marry him would hurt him more in the long term. "You love me, do you?"

His lips twitched and she reached up, wrapping her arms about his neck, needing to touch him, to be reassured that he was here, alive and well and for her. "Ye know I do. I would never have taken ye to my bed had I not meant for ye to be my wife. I was a fool not to follow ye to London, but I thought that I had lost ye. I convinced myself that the time we'd spent together had been too short for ye to fall in love with me as much as I was in love with ye."

She shook her head, weary of it all and a little sad that they'd wasted so many months wallowing in their own grief of losing each other. "How very wrong you were." Sophie could no longer wait, she leaned forward and brushed her lips against his. His hands tightened about her back and she settled against him. "I missed you too. So very much."

"And?" he asked, meeting her gaze. "Is there anything else that ye need to be telling me?"

She chuckled, supposing there was. "I love you too. I think a little part of me fell for you the moment you scooped me up in your arms on that hillside in Moy."

"Ye were very sweet in my arms, lass. I knew right then that I was in trouble and then when ye arrived at my home, I could not see straight for wanting ye. 'Tis not something I'd ever experienced before, but now that I have, 'tis a need that I'm not willing to live without."

"Neither am I," she said, kissing him fully. They came together, the kiss turning molten, and after months of being apart there would be no separating them again. Her responsibilities, her wedding flew from her thoughts as only Brice occupied her mind. They tumbled onto the bed and his deft fingers made fast work of her gown, sliding it up her hips to pool at her waist.

Sophie welcomed him, wanting him more with every minute of every day. He sat back and ripped off her pantalettes, her stockings, leaving her bare to his inspection. He watched her, his gaze dark and brimming with need and love.

She should have recognized it before she fled from Scotland for the way he was looking at her now was the same as he'd looked at her the day she had given herself to him. She'd given him her heart that day and it would seem so had he.

He kissed her, drugging her with his touch and she could not get enough. She wanted more, so much more. Sophie pushed on his shoulder until he understood and rolled onto his back. He brought her with him, and she straddled him.

She gingerly moved to take Brice into her, not sure if being with him in this way was even possible.

He shut his eyes, a whisper of a moan slipping past his lips. "That's it, lass. Take everything from me."

Sophie leaned against his chest and moved again until she found a sweet rhythm. He felt larger this way, filling and inflaming her beyond anything she'd thought possible. She would never get tired of this for it was simply heaven and to have Brice's heart made it even more perfect.

Somewhere, deep inside, he teased her closer to the peak she longed to experience again. He sat up, holding her shoulders and helping her come down on him harder. "Brice," she gasped as her body shattered around him, spiking tremor after tremor of sweet release to course through her body. She rode him, took what he gave her and kissed him as he spent within her.

Their coming together was quick and frenzied and for a few minutes they stayed as they were, waiting for their breaths and hearts to settle.

"Ye'll marry me and no one else, lass. Are we in agreement?"

She nodded, unable to form words right at that moment. She ran her hands over his cheeks, enjoying the coarse stubble that peppered his jaw. "I have to tell Mathew that I'll not be marrying him. Will ye come with me?"

His jaw hardened and his gaze cooled a little at the mention of her betrothed. "Aye. I'll come with ye. I'll not be letting ye out of my sight again."

Sophie grinned at his protectiveness or jealousy, both she would presume. "Good, because I'll not be letting you out of my sight either."

She started when a loud, insistent knock banged on her

door. "Sophie, what the hell is going on in there?" her betrothed yelled, banging again and rattling the handle.

Brice glared at the door. "Come, lass, no time like the present to tell everyone under this roof that ye're mine and I'm yers and nothing, not even a Mr. whatever his name is from wherever will change that fact."

CHAPTER 16

*B*rice stood at the side of the ballroom as his bride danced with her brother. The Marquess Graham and Louise stood next to him, talking of their impending trip to Scotland to see them once the Season ended.

They were leaving for home tomorrow and he could not wait to have Sophie back in Scotland. The only sadness to this day was that his sister had not been here to see him marry the woman he loved. But Elizabeth had practically pushed him out the door to go get her back, and so he knew she'd forgive him eventually.

"My sister is glowing, Brice. You make her happy." Louise glanced at him, smiling, and he smiled back, pleased to know he had the marquess's and marchioness's approval. After his hasty arrival last month, and his declaration on the day of Sophie's wedding that she'd not be marrying anyone other than him, he was glad he'd not done too much damage to his relationship with Sophie's family. Once they saw how happy she was, they had relented and forgiven him and then proceeded with untold enthusiasm to help organize a new wedding. One each party involved was passionate about.

"I try, my lady," he said, knowing that he'd try damn hard. At times he thought that maybe he was too eager to please, and yet he would not change. He loved her, so very much, and wanted nothing but her happiness.

The minuet came to an end and Sophie walked back over to them on her brother's arm, their laughter and her pleasure at being in their company making his lips twitch. His heart clenched and he marveled at the fact that he could adore someone as much as he adored Sophie.

His wife...

"My waltz, I believe," he said, taking her hand and kissing it. Her gaze met his and he read the need, the devotion he saw there. He knew the look well as he sported it always when about her.

She chuckled, taking his arm. "That would be my pleasure, husband."

He guided her onto the dance floor, pulling her into his arms closer than he ought. Not that he cared what the matrons of the *ton* thought of his actions. He'd hold her as close as he damn well pleased and tonight especially. It was their wedding ball that they'd wanted to hold instead of a breakfast.

"Happy?" he asked, pulling her into a spin as the music started and the dance commenced.

"Always," she said, her hand lightly playing with the tartan over his shoulder. "You look so handsome today. My very own highlander."

He stopped dancing, and, leaning down, kissed her fully, not stopping even when startled gasps and muffled laughter sounded from about the room. "And you, my dearest wife, are my very own Sassenach."

She grinned up at him, laughter in her eyes. "Not a Sassenach anymore. I'm a Scot now. Forever."

Aye, forevermore...

EPILOGUE

*S*ophie made it to the top of the hillside that she'd tumbled on two years past. She stared out over Moy and the highlands, including their own home Moy Castle, which she could just make out in the distance. "I have made it," she declared. "Two years after trying to climb this mountain, I have conquered it."

Brice came up behind her, pulling her against his chest. She wiggled into his hold, liking his warmth and strength at her back. "I would debate the term mountain, but even so, try not to fall over, lass. I'll be loath to carry ye back down again."

She turned, slapping his arm. "Tease. You enjoyed every minute of it the last time."

He grinned. "Aye, I did. In fact, it drove me mad that ye were in my arms, but ye weren't mine. Ye have a very delectable bottom, did ye know?"

"I know. You tell me often." She linked her arm in his and pulled him over to a small outcrop of rocks, before taking a seat. "I wanted to come here because this is the first place we met."

He joined her, sitting down and taking her hand, idly playing with her fingers. "Aye, it was. I canna thank your brother-in-law's carriage enough that the wheel decided to come off and strand ye here. Had it not, we would never have met."

"Hmm," Sophie said. "I think we're destined to meet our soul mates, and that no matter what, fate will play a hand and join the couples somehow. That carriage wheel was always going to come off here and we were always going to meet and you were always going to fall madly in love with me."

"I canna disagree with that last statement. 'Tis very true." He leaned over, kissing her quickly.

Sophie clasped her stomach, nerves flittering in her belly. "I wanted to bring you here today because there is something I want to tell you."

He glanced at her, a small frown marring his brow. "Are ye alright, lass? Is there something bothering ye?"

"No, nothing like that," she said, waving his concerns away. "I wanted to be here when I told you that I'm going to have your baby. You're going to be a father."

*B*rice stared at Sophie, words failing him. After two years of marriage he'd started to worry that a bairn of their own was not going to happen, and he'd accepted that fact. He loved Sophie more than anything in the world, including a child that did not exist and he'd never fret over something that he could not control.

Her words sent his mind reeling and the ground shifted under his feet a moment. "Ye are?" he managed to croak out, a lump wedged firmly in his throat.

"I am." She nodded. "The doctor confirmed it for me

when I went to town yesterday and so today you find us here, where we met and where two will soon be three."

He clasped her face, kissing her and pulling her into a fierce hug. "Oh Sophie, I dinna know what to say, other than I'm shocked, ecstatic." He pulled back, wiping the tears that spilled down her cheeks.

"You're happy then?" she asked.

He laughed, hugging her yet again. "God damn it, aye. I love ye, lass," he said, kissing her. She chuckled when he didn't stop.

"I love you too," she said, squealing when he stood quickly and swooped her up in his arms. "What are you doing?"

He started for the path and the way back down toward the village. "Carrying ye. I'll not have my pregnant wife overexerting herself and so I'll carry ye back down."

She threw him a bemused look. "If you wish. I enjoyed my little ride in your arms last time we were here. I'm more than willing to do it again."

He stopped to kiss her hard. "I enjoyed it too, lass." And he'd spend the rest of his life showing her just how much.

Dear Reader,

Thank you for taking the time to read *A Kiss in Spring*! I hope you enjoyed the third book in my Kiss the Wallflower series. Sophie was a spirited heroine who was an equal match for the Scottish hunk Brice Mackintosh. These two were easy to write as they seemed to sizzle on the page. I hope you thought so too.

I'm forever grateful to my readers, so if you're able, I would appreciate an honest review of *A Kiss in Spring*. As they say, feed an author, leave a review! You can contact me at tamaragillauthor@gmail.com or sign up to my newsletter to keep up with my writing news.

If you'd like to learn about book four in my Kiss the Wallflower series, *To Fall For a Kiss*, please read on. I have included the prologue for your reading pleasure.

Tamara Gill

TO FALL FOR A KISS

KISS THE WALLFLOWER, BOOK 4

Lady Clara Quinton is loved and admired by all. She has no enemies—excluding Mr. Stephen Grant. After an atrocious encounter with Stephen during her first season, Clara vowed to never befriend him or any member of his family. But when Mr. Grant saves her in Covent Garden from a relentless and lively admirer, Clara falters in her promise.

. . .

Disliking everything about the social sphere he now graces–including Lady Clara–Stephen wants nothing more than to steer clear of the indulged and impolite woman. Her contempt of him and his family has been made known all over the town. However, after coming to her aid one night in London, the vowed enemies come to a truce.

Now, a landlord at the property adjacent to her country estate, a storm leaves him stranded at the duke's home. Uncovering Lady Clara's secrets and vulnerabilities changes the way he sees the privileged woman. Will this newfound knowledge force him to see her through different and admiring eyes? And will Clara see there is more to Stephen than his lack of noble birth...

PROLOGUE

Covent Garden, London Season, 1809

*L*ady Clara Quinton, only daughter to the Duke of Law, gingerly backed up against an old elm tree, the laughter and sounds of gaiety beyond the garden hedge mocking her for the silly mistake she'd made. The tree bark bit into her gown and she cringed when Lord Peel would not give her space to move away.

Walking off with Viscount Peel had not been her most intelligent notion after he insisted she see a folly he was fond of. After her acquiescence, her evening had deteriorated further. If she happened to get herself out of this situation it would be the last time she'd come to Covent Garden and certainly the last time she had anything to do with his lordship.

"Please move away, my lord. You're too close."

He threw her a mocking glance, his teeth bright white under the moonlit night. His mouth reeked of spirits and she turned away, looking for anyone who may rescue her. What did he think he was going to do to her? Or get away with, the stupid man? "My lord, I must insist. My father is expecting me back at our carriage."

"Come now, Clara, we've been playing this pretty dance for years. Surely it's time for you to bestow me a kiss. I will not tell a soul. I promise."

She glanced at him. Lord Peel was a handsome man, all charm, tall, and with an abundance of friends and wealth and yet, the dance he spoke of mainly consisted of her trying to get away from him. There was something about the gentleman that made her skin crawl as if worms were slithering over her.

He'd taken an immediate like to her on the night of her debut several years ago, and she'd not been able to remove him from her side since, no matter how much she tried to show little favor to any of the men who paid her court. She was six and twenty and sole heir to her father's many estates. She wanted for nothing, and with so many other things occupying her mind of late, a husband did not fit in with her plans at present.

If she were to marry she would have to leave her father, and she could not do that. Not now when he was so very ill and in all honesty, there had been no one who had sparked her interest, not since Marquess Graham during her coming out year before he up and married a servant. Clara would be lying if she had not felt slighted and confused by his choice.

"If you should try and kiss me, my lord, I shall tell my father of your conduct. I can promise you that. Now move." She pushed at his shoulders and she may as well have been pushing against a log of wood. He didn't budge, simply leaned in closer, clasping her chin and squashing her farther into the tree trunk. She cringed at the pain he induced.

"Do not make me force you, Clara." His voice dropped to a deep whisper full of menace.

Fear rippled through her and she shivered, glancing

beyond his shoulder. Should she scream? To do so would court scandal. People would come scrambling to her aid, and she would be left having to explain why she was alone with Lord Peel in the first place. Especially if they did not have an understanding. Clara could not put her father through such gossip. He had enough on his shoulders without her worrying him with her own mistakes.

"You're a brute. How dare you treat me like this?" She tried to move away once again and as quick as a flash he grabbed her, wresting her to the ground. She did scream then, but with his chest over her face her cry for help was muffled.

Clara pushed at him as he tried to kiss her, his hands hard and rough against her face. "Stop," she said, "please stop."

He merely laughed, the sound mocking, and then in an instant he was gone. For a moment she remained on the ground, trying to figure out what had happened and then she saw him. Mr. Grant, or Stephen Grant, the Marquess Graham's brother-in-law and a man she'd promised to loathe forever and a day. He stood over Lord Peel, his face a mixture of horror and fury. Somewhere in the commotion Mr. Grant must have punched Lord Peel, for he was holding his jaw and there was a small amount of blood on his lip.

Clara scrambled to her feet, wiping at her gown and removing the grass and garden debris from her dress as best she could. Mr. Grant came to her, clasping her shoulders and giving her a little shake. "Are you injured? Did he hurt you at all?"

Clara glanced at Lord Peel as he gained his feet. He glared at Mr. Grant as he too wiped garden debris from his clothing and righted his superfine coat.

"You may leave, Mr. Grant. You're not welcome to intrude in a private conversation I'm having with Lady Clara."

"Private? Mauling someone on the ground is not what I'd consider a conversation, my lord. I heard her shout for assistance. I hardly think the conversation was one of Lady Clara's liking."

Clara moved over toward Mr. Grant when Lord Peel took a menacing step in her direction. An odd thing for her to do as she had never been friends with the man and to seek his protection now went against everything within her. But if she were to remain at Lord Peel's mercy, she would choose Mr. Grant of course. He had two sisters after all, and from what she'd seen over the years he loved them dearly. He would not allow any harm to come to her. Mr. Grant reached out a hand and shuffled her behind him, backing her toward where her father would be waiting with the carriage.

Lord Peel's eyes blazed with anger. "Of course it was to her liking. We're courting, you fool."

She gasped, stepping forward, but Mr. Grant clasped her about the waist and held her back. "How dare you, my lord?" she stated even as Mr. Grant restrained her. "I never once asked for you to pursue me and I never gave you any indication that I wanted you to."

Lord Peel glared at her. Mr. Grant turned her back toward the opening in the hedge where they had entered the small, private space and pushed her on. "Go, Lady Clara. I shall speak to his lordship. I can watch from here to ensure you reach your carriage, which if I'm not mistaken your father is waiting beside and looking for you."

Clara clasped Mr. Grant's hands, squeezing them. "I cannot thank you enough. You have proven to be the best kind of man for coming to the aid of a woman you may not be inclined to help under normal circumstances. I thank you for it."

He threw her a puzzled glance. "Should anyone bellow for help and I hear it, of course I will come. Now go, Lady

Clara. The time apart from your guests has been long enough."

Clara nodded, turning and walking away. She reached up and fixed her hair, hoping it did not look as out of place as it felt. As she walked back toward the revelers, a little of her fear slipped away knowing Mr. Grant watched her. She glanced over her shoulder, and true to his word, Mr. Grant continued to survey her progress and ensure she arrived back at her carriage safely.

A shiver of awareness slid over her skin, completely opposite to what she experienced each time she was in the presence of Lord Peel. She'd always disliked Mr. Grant and his siblings, one of whom married Marquess Graham, her own suitor during her first Season and the man she thought she would marry. He did not offer for her hand, choosing to marry a lady's companion instead.

"There you are, my dear. I've been looking for you."

She reached up and kissed her father's cheek, her legs of a sudden feeling as if they would not hold her for too much longer. "Shall we go, Papa?" she said, taking his arm and guiding him toward the carriage. The coachman bowed before opening the door for them.

"Yes, let us go, my dear. I've had quite enough time in the gardens and watching the *ton* at play."

Clara stepped up into the carriage and sank down on the padded velvet seats, relief pouring through her that no one other than Mr. Grant had come upon her and his lordship in the garden, or the position that they'd been found.

Heat rushed over her cheeks and she picked up the folded blanket on her seat and settled it about her father's legs as the carriage lurched forward. Anything to distract her from the memory of it.

"Shall we ring for tea and play a game of chess when we

arrive home, Papa? It may be a nice way to end the evening just us two together."

Her father glanced at her, a little blank and unsure. "I think I shall retire, my dear. It's been a tiring evening."

"Very well," she said, swallowing the lump in her throat that wedged there each and every time she was around her parent. She knew the reason he no longer liked to play chess, cards or even the piano, at which he'd once been proficient, was because he'd forgotten how. His mind over the last two years had slowly disremembered many things, even some of the servants who had been with them since she was a girl.

Unbeknownst to her father Clara had sought out an opinion with their family doctor and he'd agreed that her father had become more forgetful and vague, and that it may be a permanent affliction.

She sighed. The fact that there was little she could do to help him regain his memory saddened her and as much as she tried to remind him of things, an awful realization that one day he'd forget her had lodged in her brain and would not dissipate.

What would happen after that? Would he still be as healthy as he was now, but with no memory, or would whatever this disease that ailed his mind affect his body as well.

The idea was not to be borne. He was all she had left.

"Maybe tomorrow, Papa, after breakfast perhaps."

He smiled at her, and she grinned back. "Maybe, my dear, or you could ask your mother. I know how very fond of chess she is."

Clara nodded, blinking and looking out the carriage window so he would not see her upset. If only she could ask her mama, who'd been dead these past ten years.

*S*tephen stood between Lord Peel and the man's exit at his back in the gardens. The moment he'd strode into the small, private area and seen a flash of pink muslin and a gentleman forcing a woman into kissing him a veil of red had descended over his eyes and he'd not known how he'd stopped himself from pummeling the man into pulp.

"You will leave Lady Clara alone or I shall speak to her father of what I witnessed this evening. Do you understand, my lord?"

Peel chuckled, the sound mocking and full of an arrogance that Stephen was well aware of with this gentleman. He was also aware that he'd once been married and that his wife had fallen ill not long after their marriage. Of course, upon the young woman's death, Peel had played the widower very well, and had enjoyed the copious amount of money that his young wife had left him, or so Marquess Graham had told him one evening when Stephen had noticed his marked attention toward Lady Clara. A woman who seemed to show little interest in the gentleman trying to court her.

Lord Peel tapped a finger against his chin. "I forget… Do I need to listen to you? What is your name… Mr. Grant, isn't it? Son of nobody."

Stephen fisted his hands at his sides, reminding himself that to break the fellow's nose would not do him or his sisters any good now that they were part of the sphere this mongrel resided within. He'd already hit him once, to bloody him up too much would not do.

"You are correct. I'm Mr. Stephen Grant of Nobody of Great Import, but I will say this… You're no one of import either if the rumors about you and your conduct are to be believed."

Lord Peel's face mottled red and Stephen was glad his words struck a chord in the bastard. He needed to hear some truths and to know that his marked attention toward women, his inability to grasp that he saw them as nothing but playthings for his enjoyment had been noted and talked about. He pushed past Stephen and he let him go, not wanting to waste another moment of his time on such a nob.

The gentleman's retreating footsteps halted. "Lady Clara will be my wife. I will be speaking to her father soon about my proposal and I will have her. I am a viscount. It is only right that Lady Clara marry a man such as myself, so if you look to her as a possible candidate as your wife, you'll be sadly mistaken. Move on and marry a tavern wench, that'll suit your status better. A duke's daughter is not for you."

Stephen glared at the man's back as he disappeared into the throng of revelers still dancing and enjoying their night in Covent Garden. "Yes, well, Lord Peel, she's not for you either and I'll be damned if I'll let you have her."

LORDS OF LONDON SERIES
AVAILABLE NOW!

Dive into these charming historical romances! In this six-book series by Tamara Gill, Darcy seduces a virginal duke, Cecilia's world collides with a roguish marquess, Katherine strikes a deal with an unlucky earl and Lizzy sets out to conquer a very wicked Viscount. These stories plus more adventures in the Lords of London series!

LEAGUE OF UNWEDDABLE GENTLEMEN SERIES AVAILABLE NOW!

Fall into my latest series, where the heroines have to fight for what they want, both regarding their life and love. And where the heroes may be unweddable to begin with, that is until they meet the women who'll change their fate. The League of Unweddable Gentlemen series is available now!

ALSO BY TAMARA GILL

Royal House of Atharia Series

TO DREAM OF YOU

A ROYAL PROPOSITION

FOREVER MY PRINCESS

League of Unweddable Gentlemen Series

TEMPT ME, YOUR GRACE

HELLION AT HEART

DARE TO BE SCANDALOUS

TO BE WICKED WITH YOU

KISS ME DUKE

THE MARQUESS IS MINE

Kiss the Wallflower series

A MIDSUMMER KISS

A KISS AT MISTLETOE

A KISS IN SPRING

TO FALL FOR A KISS

A DUKE'S WILD KISS

TO KISS A HIGHLAND ROSE

KISS THE WALLFLOWER - BOOKS 1-3 BUNDLE

Lords of London Series

TO BEDEVIL A DUKE

TO MADDEN A MARQUESS

TO TEMPT AN EARL

TO VEX A VISCOUNT

TO DARE A DUCHESS

TO MARRY A MARCHIONESS

LORDS OF LONDON - BOOKS 1-3 BUNDLE

LORDS OF LONDON - BOOKS 4-6 BUNDLE

To Marry a Rogue Series

ONLY AN EARL WILL DO

ONLY A DUKE WILL DO

ONLY A VISCOUNT WILL DO

ONLY A MARQUESS WILL DO

ONLY A LADY WILL DO

A Time Traveler's Highland Love Series

TO CONQUER A SCOT

TO SAVE A SAVAGE SCOT

TO WIN A HIGHLAND SCOT

Time Travel Romance

DEFIANT SURRENDER

A STOLEN SEASON

Scandalous London Series

A GENTLEMAN'S PROMISE

A CAPTAIN'S ORDER

A MARRIAGE MADE IN MAYFAIR

SCANDALOUS LONDON - BOOKS 1-3 BUNDLE

High Seas & High Stakes Series

HIS LADY SMUGGLER

HER GENTLEMAN PIRATE

HIGH SEAS & HIGH STAKES - BOOKS 1-2 BUNDLE

Daughters Of The Gods Series
BANISHED-GUARDIAN-FALLEN
DAUGHTERS OF THE GODS - BOOKS 1-3 BUNDLE

Stand Alone Books
TO SIN WITH SCANDAL
OUTLAWS

ABOUT THE AUTHOR

Tamara is an Australian author who grew up in an old mining town in country South Australia, where her love of history was founded. So much so, she made her darling husband travel to the UK for their honeymoon, where she dragged him from one historical monument and castle to another.

A mother of three, her two little gentlemen in the making, a future lady (she hopes) and a part-time job keep her busy in the real world, but whenever she gets a moment's peace she loves to write romance novels in an array of genres, including regency, medieval and time travel.

www.tamaragill.com
tamaragillauthor@gmail.com

Printed in Great Britain
by Amazon